Pride Publishing books by KD Ellis

Out in Austin
Teddy's Truth
Shiloh's Secret
Trusting Tennyson
Loving Lennox

Demon Daddy
The Blood Demon's Pet

I0607649

Demon Daddy

THE BLOOD DEMON'S PET

KD ELLIS

The Blood Demon's Pet
ISBN # 978-1-80250-578-8
©Copyright KD Ellis 2023
Cover Art by Kelly Martin ©Copyright November 2023
Interior text design by Claire Siemaszkiewicz
Pride Publishing

Published in 2023 by Pride Publishing, United Kingdom.

Pride Publishing is an imprint of Totally Entwined Group Limited.

THE BLOOD DEMON'S PET

Dedication

To Elaine, who is TOO YOUNG to read this book,
Put it back until you can legally drink.
I'm watching you...
But their love of all things fantasy and paranormal
Reinspired my own joy in the genre.
So thanks...
Someday I'll let you read this.
Maybe.

Chapter One

Eryn

My room is cold.

Not just the bitter cold of winter — though it *is* that, too — but a lonely sort, a chill that starts in my chest and spreads outward. My breath flickers like a specter on the windowpane before turning to frost. I scuff it away with my forearm so I can peer through the yellowed glass.

Two shadowy figures are standing on the wilting lawn, but I know Alpha Carrick must be the one by the porch. I can only see the top of his head, with its shiny bald patch glinting up at me, but I don't think Alpha would let a stranger between him and his pack.

Alpha's shoulders are stiff — tense and strong.

I wonder what he's saying. If he would turn toward the window, I could read his lips. Instead, I'm stuck interpreting his body language.

The other man steps away, shaking his head. His dark hair flops over his face, but I notice the way his lips turn down. Alpha moves forward, but the stranger lifts his hand. He slashes it sharply across his chest in an obvious refusal. I don't need to see any more. My shoulders slump as I twist away from the window.

I've been passed over.

Again.

I wilt against the glass and let my bare feet thump against the wall just *one* time. A single show of disappointment before I swallow it down. It's sour on my tongue, like the sugar-free lemonade Alpha's mate serves at summer's end.

I'm not surprised. Most packs are overpopulated now, with the laws dictating where we can settle. Well, where we can settle *if* we want to be able to shift freely, anyway. I'm not an Omega—one of the rare male wolves able to bear pups—and I'm not particularly smart or strong. I'd be having a hard time even if I *wasn't* a freak.

Maybe I should give up, accept that I'm destined to be on my own. It won't be the first time. I don't need a pack, because lone wolves survived in the wild. I just need...

I close my eyes, trying to find my inner wolf. He's there, somewhere, pacing under my skin, antsy and rabid—a growling mutt. But even though I can feel him, I can't *touch* him. My ribs could be silver bars, as well as they keep the beast caged.

Caged, but not docile.

I slide off the windowsill and dart to the bed, the wooden floor icy under my soles. I dive under the comforter before grabbing my pillow, dragging it over my face so I can scream into the sheets as the beast growls at me, snapping his jaws in threat.

The phantom press of his claws digs into my fingertips. I curl my fingers toward my palms without thinking. They slice into my skin like shattered glass. At least the pain distracts me from the ache in my teeth. I can smell *everything* — the forest through the window, out of reach, the bleeding meat in the fridge, the salt of Alpha's sweat.

Trying to tame my inner wolf is as useless as asking my shadow to dance. Neither listen.

I manage to choke down my scream just as Alpha's heavy boots hit the stairs and start climbing. My door whines as it swings open.

"You up, kid?" Alpha Carrick's voice is deep as thunder. As much as I'd like to ignore him, I know he can hear my ragged breathing. I shove my hand out from under the pillow and give a half-hearted thumbs up. It won't be the first time Alpha has seen my hands covered in blood, and I doubt it will be the last. At least this time, it's my own.

My feral wolf never bothered learning to submit, not even to me.

Alpha is quiet, but then the mattress dips under his weight. I slap my hand against the sheets to keep from sliding into him. Alpha awkwardly pats my back. "I don't think that pack is going to be a good fit for you. Alpha Reed is…old-fashioned."

"I saw through the window." My voice is muffled by the pillow. "He didn't want me. You don't have to lie."

"It's not that he didn't want *you*. He just doesn't have the resources to…" Alpha hesitates so I fill in the blanks for him.

"To babysit a freak." I barely have the words out of my mouth before Alpha slips his hand under the pillow. He pinches my ear and drags me out like an unruly pup, ignoring my yelp.

"You are *not* a freak." Alpha does that thing that all adults do—say something that isn't true, then expect me to believe them. Because for some reason, adults are allowed to lie if it's for your own good.

I'm an adult now. I sit up and cross my arms over my scrawny chest—too small, too wimpy…a runt not even worthy of belonging to a litter.

"I *am* a freak. Everybody says it." Even *she'd* said it, the woman in my dreams. I can't remember her face, but I know she smelled of nicotine and mint, and when she sang, her voice was gritty. And I remember she had kind hands.

Until she didn't.

"If everybody said aconite tastes like cotton candy, would you eat it?" Alpha's question is pointed, his voice cross.

"Maybe. At least then no one would have to put up with me." My jaw juts out stubbornly as I lie.

Alpha cuffs the back of my head. "Eryn Laurier, don't disrespect me with words like that." He grips my nape tightly, forcing my face up to meet his pale eyes. They are stern but kind, lined from years of laughter. "I don't 'put up' with anything I don't want to, and I certainly don't 'put up' with you, kid."

"I'm *not* a kid." I shove my hair out of my face. If I were a kid, I wouldn't have to leave. If I were a kid, the last pack run wouldn't have ruined everything. Instead, at nineteen, I was too old for my wolf's antics to be excused. A wolf who couldn't submit was a wolf who couldn't stay.

The mattress creaks as Alpha stands. He gives a heavy sigh as he walks. I barely hear him mutter, "I guess you're not."

I want to retreat to the safety of my pillows. Hide away from reality and let it pass me by like an autumn storm, but there are chores to be done before dusk falls tomorrow.

* * * *

Goddess Moon hangs pregnant in the sky. Around me, the woods echo with the sound of breaking bones and shifting skin. I watch Old Jeb fall to his knees, his skin rippling over unnaturally bent joints. He makes it look easy, the transition from man to beast happening in an instant. His wolf, with its shaggy, silver-streaked hair, trots off into the woods, snapping at a teenager caught mid-transition, fur sprouting in clumps over his lumpy spine.

Alpha said it takes bravery for a wolf to submit to the pull of the Goddess so fully. That only the strongest wolves, like the pack Beta, who is already shaking out his dark fur, can change so quickly. But only the oldest can resist the pull entirely, like Alpha Carrick.

And me, but not because I'm strong.

Because I'm weak.

Like the rest of the pack, I stand naked in the clearing. The grass, stiff with frost and its color faded, pricks the soles of my feet. I can no longer fight off the shivers. They come, one right after another, until it feels like I'm having a seizure. My blond hair is long enough to tickle my hipbones but does little to shield me from the cold, not even when I curl forward, clasping my arms tight around my waist for warmth. A breeze whispers along the shell of my ear. And the light—

Goddess Moon's light does nothing but paint my pale skin in tones of blue. I feel nothing…just the beast, pacing in my belly. I try to reach it like Alpha says, to put a leash on its neck and drag it into the light. Again, he cowers from me, snapping his jaws in threat.

A frustrated growl slides between my flat, clenched teeth.

Alpha grips the nape of my neck, the only point of warmth in the winter night. "Take a deep breath."

I know it will be pointless, but I gasp one in. The cold air hits my lungs like a lit match.

"Good boy. Now another," Alpha guides me through taking the breaths as slow and deep as I can, despite my body's shaking. Each breath helps a bit more. The cold leeches away until all I feel is numb. The only thing keeping me from melting into a puddle of mercury is the weight of his palm.

Goddess Moon glints through the bare branches above me. Alpha tightens his hand on my neck, his claws scraping my skin where they push through his fleshy fingertips. His voice is deeper now, guttural under her sway. I can tell he's fighting to stay out of her riptide long enough to talk me through this, like he always does.

He is a good Alpha. Even though my wolf doesn't accept him, Alpha still takes care of me. He doesn't lock me in the kennel like *she* used to or drag me down to the lake to…to… I clench my eyes shut and concentrate on anything but the memory.

It feels like hours—like days—but finally, I feel the itch of fur stirring under my flesh. My knees collapse, and I strike the dirt with a cry. The shift is agonizing. I can hear myself screaming as my bones break and mend and rearrange. Skin tears then knits itself back together, sensitive as a sunburn. Twice, the shift tries to revert as I cringe away from the pain, but Alpha growls an order to push through, dragging my wolf from under my skin by his scruff.

Finally, it's over.

The pain becomes a hollow parody. I slowly push myself up onto four paws, my spine popping. Handfuls of fur finish sprouting, and I whine at the overwhelming need to scratch the itchy pelt.

My gait is awkward, a halting stumble toward the woods where the rest of the wolves are already running. Alpha overtakes me quickly. He is twice my size, his fur brindled. The other wolves are quick to move out of his way.

For a moment—just a brief stretch of lucid seconds—I think that this pack run will be different.

I feel my mind blurring at the edges and panic sets in. I whine when my beast shoulders me out of the way, stumbling when he briefly takes control of my forelegs. I struggle to leash him, to keep him chained to my will. In this body, he is stronger than me. The beast growls, the sound rumbling from my chest, and instinctively, my mind cowers back, giving ground before it.

It is a mistake. I don't know why my wolf is so much wilder than the rest of the pack, why he won't bend to my will as he should. Instead, he tamps me down, burying me under the instinct to run, to hunt and claim. It feels like falling asleep, but each month, I slip under easier.

One day, I'm afraid I won't wake up.

Chapter Two

Eryn

I wake up alone, covered in blood and clumps of feathers. The carcass of a bird — a turkey, I think, from the plumage — is scattered detritus around me. My mouth is dry, and when I cough, I spit out several quills. They float into the air like pillow down. The sun is creeping up the sky but it does little to warm my naked body. I groan at the thought of walking back to the pack house.

At least if I lose a toe or two, they'll grow back after Goddess Moon's next visit. It is the only benefit to the painful shift. The real issue isn't the potential for frostbite.

I have no idea where I am.

The forest on pack land is as familiar to me as a nursery rhyme. I could go years without hearing it — weeks without traveling its paths — and it always comes back to me like instinct. The land is steeped in history, generations of wolves leaving their markings on every stone and blade of grass.

These trees are strangers, their scent foreign. I stand and spin in a slow circle, hoping I'm wrong, hoping that one tree out of thousands will look familiar and point me in the right direction. I don't know what to do, where to start. Any direction I pick could be wrong, leading me farther from the safety of the pack and closer to the dangers of humanity.

Or worse, since humans are far from the most dangerous thing out here. They were only one of the horror stories I heard at bedtime. A shiver crawls down my spine as I realize just how vulnerable I really am, out here alone in the woods — to the elements, to the so-called hunters who shoot first and ask questions later.

And to the Bloodwraiths.

A pitiful whine leaks from my lips at the thought. I'd overheard one of the older boys talking about them when I was younger, and no amount of reassurance from Alpha could convince me that they were a myth. If humans are real, with their gunpowder and blades, and wixxes with their spells and potions, then why not Bloodwraiths?

Demons who feast on the blood of their victims, like vampires but stronger and faster. The other boys said they could rip the arteries from an enemy's body in the space of a heartbeat and that a single Bloodwraith could decimate an entire army.

I still have nightmares from the single, solitary dinner I'd had to sit through with the Kiss of Vampires that live in the neighboring territory, and the worst they'd done was smile with their cloudy dead eyes.

Something snaps in the distance to my right, and I yelp, literally jumping as I spin toward the noise.

Between barren trees and shadow, I see nothing, just wood and grass. Still, it makes up my mind. I walk in the other direction.

I drag in a deep breath, but only my scent surrounds me, giving no clue if I'm going the right direction. Each noise makes me jump, and I curse my weakness, especially when I step on a sharp stone and the pain startles a cry out of me. The noise echoes through the woods, disturbing a flock of sparrows nesting in a nearby tree.

I instinctively duck, flapping my hands around my head, then feel silly. At least there's no one around to see me. Then again, if there was, I could ask them for directions. Slowly, I straighten.

Through some stroke of luck, the kind that normally doesn't happen to me, the wind changes. It is still bitterly cold, and I shiver, but it brings with it a familiar scent. Though faded, I can still follow it, drifting in from the north. I start walking. I can tell just from its faintness that I am quite a distance away. My wolf can travel farther on four feet than I can on two.

I hate that he has stranded me here.

At least the woods are less scary now, with a clear direction to follow.

Several hours later, I curse my wolf out loud. Being able to shift reliably would be *super* convenient right about now. The sun is sinking in the sky, my feet are shredded and I think my dick is trying to climb into my body from the cold. I want to sit down, but I know from experience that if I do, my feet will hurt even worse when I stand back up.

Finally, sometime near dinnertime—or what my stomach loudly yells at me *should* be dinnertime, if I was willing to take my wolf's suggestion to eat fowl—I stumble onto a path that *looks* familiar. I can't wait to get back to the pack house where hopefully, there will still be something left from the after-run meal. If I don't find something to eat soon, I think my stomach might literally try to eat me from the inside out, it's growling so loud.

I smell the property line before I see it. The sentries patrol it often, marking trees at random. The scent of urine is overpowering, but I've never been more grateful for its presence. I barely cross it when a large black wolf trots out in front of me, its teeth bared. A threatening growl tears from his throat, and I drop to the ground, ignoring the twigs that stab into my flesh. I roll onto my back, my belly exposed, and lift my jaw to bare my throat.

My human body is smart enough to submit.

After the initial warning, the wolf is silent in his approach. Of all the members of the pack, Beta scares me the most—not because of his size, though he is larger than most, but because of his eyes. They follow me, always watching, always waiting for me to mess up. From the glint in them, I know I've really done it now.

He plants his forepaw on the center of my chest, the weight pinning me down so that even if I wanted to move, I couldn't. A whine leaks from my lips, unbidden. Then it is not his paw on my chest but his hand, digging his nails into my skin.

"Naughty boy. The whole pack is out looking for you," Beta chides. His face is wrong—twisted, almost manic. "And after what you did to Alpha." He shakes his head like he's disappointed but he's not. His delight is easy to see.

"Alpha?" I ask, skirting my eyes toward the pack house, still out of sight. "What happened? Is he okay? What...what did I do?" I remember nothing. If my memories are a scrapbook, last night is an empty page—blank, just a long stretch of rolling blackness.

Beta looks surprised that I need to ask, though he shouldn't be. The entire pack knows of my deficiency. My wolf is feral, a wild animal that takes control once a month. "You attacked him, Eryn. Tore his throat open."

A cold sweat coats my skin. The pull of the Goddess Moon might force the normally controllable shift, but she also brings with her advanced healing abilities. Under her light, we are nearly invincible. But even Goddess Moon can't fix *some* things.

"I didn't. I *wouldn't*," I protest, my heart quickening. Alpha is the only one in the pack who cares for me, even if only in his own way. I don't remember much about the day I was dropped off on the outskirts of pack property as a pup, dirty and malnourished, but I've heard the story enough.

About how several mated pairs had been willing to foster me at first, until they realized I was broken. Everyone wanted a pup, but no one wanted a pup who couldn't shift, a pup who feared footsteps and water and dark places, a pup who whined through the day and howled all night.

I'm surprised none of *them* had tried to drown me.

It was a rough time and mostly my memories of it are disjointed, flashes of moments threaded together with feelings of fear and confusion.

"But you did." Beta shakes his head, looking disappointed. "I was rooting for you, kid. Really thought you'd fit in eventually."

"I... Alpha understands my problem," I say, mostly to myself. "I *wouldn't* attack him. I wouldn't."

"Oh, but you did. They found him in the lilies, your scent all over him. The pack's called for a tribunal." Beta sounds sympathetic but his eyes prove the lie. I don't know why he hates me, except that Alpha always gives me attention he sees as owed to him instead. It shouldn't matter. I'm not a threat to his position.

I finally sit up, wrapping my arms around my chest. "I wouldn't do that."

Would I?

I start to shake, this time not from the cold.

Beta pats my arm. "Don't worry. I bet they'll make it quick."

It doesn't help. It almost makes it worse. As much as dying will fuck up my life, killing me will probably hurt the pack just as much. They might be cold and distant, but they were still family, still my pack.

"Can't..." I suck in a breath, fear filling me like a clogged pipe, overflowing into my body. My breath comes out in a gasp. "Will you do it?" I don't like Beta, and he doesn't like me. He won't mind. Killing me will be easy, a chore to do quickly, then forget about.

If my death can't be painless for me, I'd rather it be painless for the pack.

Beta smiles like he's trying to comfort me, but I don't trust it. It makes him look more wolffish than ever. "I can do that, if that's what you want—or I can help you leave. I'll tell the tribunal I didn't see you, and eventually, people will forget."

"Leave? Where would I go?" I flinch at the thought. Would he take me to live with the humans? Without Alpha to talk me through my shift, what will happen? When I was younger, before joining the pack, I'd fought the shift and the pain was unbearable. Can I go through that again, month after month?

If enduring the pain means not dying?

I nod slowly. "I don't have my clothes…or money. I don't know where to go."

"Let me handle that. Wait here and stay out of sight. I'll be back." Beta shifts to his wolf and pads away. I curl my arms tighter around myself like somehow, that will keep the fear inside.

Chapter Three

Master

The Flesh Market is busy.

I hate the breath of the living on my skin. It reeks of rotted meat and compost—and too often of fear, and that's not even considering the sweat and dirt and chemical perfumes they insist on dousing their bodies with. I should have come last night, but Lucifer was being a needy bitch.

I'll have to shower when I get back.

If only today weren't the last day the market will be in the area. Unfortunately, I can't wait weeks for it to replenish its stock and come back around. I *might* have been a bit too careless with my last feeder.

I know better than to wait this long—or at least I should know by now. I'd be lucky if there is any good stock left, but I seriously hate grocery shopping. How am I supposed to know what I'll feel like for dinner next week? Some days I crave pixies with their light, fruity taste. Sometimes I'd prefer the spicy tang of a dragon. Asking me to pick beforehand just really isn't fair.

I'd tried getting more than one feeder at a time before, but for some reason, they always ended up killing each other.

It didn't used to be so annoying, before the internet and social media and, of course, the formation of the BAA. The Bureau of Arcane Activity has a real stick up their ass about the little things — like unregistered familiars and eating people. They can't stop me from feeding, of course. I have the right to live just like every other creature, but the paperwork for an accidental draining is *murder*. I miss the old ways.

Mostly on grocery shopping days.

At least the market has set the enclosures up with enough room to maneuver between them this time. The chain-link pens are separated, as always, by species. After all, it would be stupid to stable a Unicorn near an Ankhuban. The lust the Ankhuban stirs up in buyers would traumatize the Unicorn, and nobody wants to buy a one with a curdled horn.

I glance in several pens as I stroll through the market. As I fear, most are empty. The few creatures left aren't my preferred taste, but I have no one to blame but myself. In the nearest pen, a centaur stands with his ass to the fence, flicking his tail in either annoyance or boredom. I slow to admire his physique but don't stop. My Nightmares would never stoop to sharing their stables, and even if they did, I'm not in the mood for horse.

In the next pen, a Brownie huddles in the corner, his thin shirt clearly not enough to protect him from the early winter air. The two black X's tattooed on his forehead move me along quickly. Bad enough to get stuck with a criminal for dinner, let alone a repeat offender.

It takes a special kind of stupid to sign a work contract with a Flesh Market. The million-dollar payout at the end of the contract can only be cashed out if you survive, and no amount of money can buy your body back if its damaged. And criminals didn't even get *that*. They just got a reduced sentence.

If it were me, I'd rather do ten years in solitary than one as a slave. But, hey…to each their own, right?

Not, of course, that *I'd* ever end up in that position. They'd have to catch me in the first place. I snort at the thought, ignoring the flinch another buyer makes at the sound. Sprites are such flighty beings.

My eyes meet the glare of a siren as I pass, and it's heated enough to make me pause. Their gaze is harsh, and I can feel them weaving their magic around me, enticing me closer. Or trying to… It would take a dozen such as them to make me so much as blink against my will. I move closer all on my own, curiosity growing at their audacity.

Like many of the others in the pen, they have a black X tattooed on their forehead. The siren's split tongue flicks out of their mouth to wet their lips. Their voice is raspy as they speak. "If the nights grow cold and lonely, sailor, let me warm your bed."

I grin, exposing my dagger-like incisors. "Does the ocean flow in your veins, Sea Witch?" They hiss at the old term, their eyes flashing blue. Their kind and mine have a complicated history, a tangled web of alliances and war.

"Demon," they accuse, dipping their chin in insult.

"It's been an age since I've tasted your kind." I look them up and down. Time has not been kind to their people. Skin once smooth and crisp like the sea is now saggy and brittle. After the melting of the ice caps in the mid twenty-first century then the fallout from increased fracking just prior to the Collapse, much of the sirens' territories have been destroyed. Last I'd heard, most had taken to the land, cutting themselves off from their magic in exchange for survival.

From the state of this one, I don't think they've fully left the sea. They are not broken *enough*. It's a pity that I'm not feeling seafood. "If only you had a dick." I sigh and give them one last look. Like all sirens, they are androgynous. I have a brief curiosity about what gender they've chosen, if any.

Maybe I'll purchase their contract anyway, if I don't find anything suitable. I prefer males but...any port in a storm.

I snicker at the pun as I leave them behind, ignoring their loud screech of anger.

None of the other pens reveal anything better. After nearly an hour of wandering, I'm resigned to either the siren or the centaur.

A second round through the market puts the sun high over my head but leaves me no closer to finding a better feeder, so I make my way toward the familiar red tent at the edge of the market. One side is held open by gold tassels. It is gaudy and completely unnecessary in a place like this. I have the urge to yank on the rope, but I restrain myself. I deserve a medal.

The bursar is a jinni I've met several times, but his name slips my mind. His lower half is a tornado of blue smoke, loose papers and dust motes trapped in the swirl. He is hovering on one side of a heavy desk. I can only see the backs of the two people sitting across from him.

Both wolves, but one is larger than the other, hair dark. His shoulders dwarf the tiny chair he sits in. The other is practically a child beside him, though I know they must be legal to be at the Market. All I can see is the nearly white hair hanging over their shoulders.

Probably a female, from its length, which is a pity. She smells delicious. I've heard many a vampire comparing the smell of blood to their favorite food when they were human—apple pie or strawberries, once even heroin. I've never found mortal food to smell like anything but chemicals and rot.

If I were forced to describe it, I'd say the wolf smells like moonlight and ivy.

The bursar grabs the contract from the smaller wolf's hand and skims the signature before a greedy smile creeps over his face. "Welcome to the Flesh Market, Mr. Laurier." The jinni snaps his fingers and a hulking male who looks human but smells of honeysuckle—Fae, if I ever smelled one—ducks under the flap of the tent.

The Jinni waves to the blond. "Have him prepped for the auction."

Him? My gaze sharpens on the small figure as the Fae drags him out of his chair with a firm grip on his upper arm. The boy yelps, turning to the larger wolf beside him, who stays seated. The move gives me a good look at his pretty face.

He seems young. His skin is pale and smooth, only a hint of scruff giving him away as an adult. His blue eyes are wide with fear. "Beta?" he cries, trying to pull his arm free.

"Go with the nice men, Eryn." The older wolf is clearly amused at the younger one's plight, and he isn't bothering to hide it. I don't particularly care about whatever drama brought the two here. A debt to settle, a crime to pay for, it's all the same to me.

"Wait." I step farther into the tent before the Fae can continue out. A knowing gleam sparks in the jinni's eyes. *Niall, that's his name*, I finally remember. I've been doing business with him for too long for him to not know my type. It's just rather unfortunate that my type so rarely ends up in the pens. "Skip the auction, and I'll add ten percent to the usual fee."

"Levi, my good friend, I'd love to help you out, you know that." Niall's voice is slick as an oil spill as he floats right through the desk, ignoring the mess he leaves behind. "But this one is *special*."

I turn to the boy, examining him with a calculating eye. "He looks cleaner than the others, that's true." I reach out and grip the boy's chin, tipping his face this way and that. Except for a few scratches on his cheek, he's flawless. Mr. Laurier, Niall called him. The larger wolf called him Eryn. If I have my way, he'll be called *Pet*. He doesn't protest my handling, but his eyes keep darting back to the wolf he called Beta.

"Not just cleaner. Fresh meat. Untouched, in *every* way. Isn't that right, boy?" Niall hovers at the young man's back, close enough his wind stirs the boy's hair, and stares pointedly at my hand until I reluctantly remove it.

My future pet swallows. I watch his throat tense around the motion, his skin tightening over his larynx before he gives a brief nod. "Yes, sir."

"So you see, friend or not, he's worth well more than a measly ten percent." Niall fingers the oversized white shirt hanging off the boy's shoulder and the boy shudders, cringing away. I smirk. He'd not resisted *my* touch.

I let my fangs show. "I'll pay double the fee and triple the opening bid."

Niall looks like he's considering it, but then he shrugs and shakes his head. "You'll have to go to the auction like everyone else. This little gem is going to be my crown jewel. Get him cleaned up, Ronan."

Niall nods to the honeysuckle Fae, who drags the boy out of the tent. He looks back over his shoulder for just a second before he vanishes around the corner. Faintly, I hear a rumbling, like quaking earth threatening to split, before I realize the sound is coming from my chest and I cut it off abruptly. I leave the bursar behind, no longer willing to settle for a siren when I can play with a wolf instead.

Chapter Four

Eryn

I try to catch one last look at Beta before I am dragged out of the tent, but my eyes don't make it past the dark-haired stranger. *Levi,* his name whispers in my mind. I can still feel his aura pressing against my skin, heavy and dangerous, even once he's out of sight. He isn't a wolf but that doesn't bring me closer to telling what he is. I'd learned about the most common species growing up, but except for when I was a young pup, I rarely get to meet non-wolves in person. I met a wix once, when she redid the wards around the pack lands, but that was only for a moment.

She had pink hair.

I don't have time to dwell on the stranger. The man gripping my arm drags me to another tent, smaller than the red one where Beta had explained the work contract that he wanted me to sign. It didn't seem too bad, a few years of working in exchange for a roof over my head and food in my belly. He said it didn't even matter that

I don't have experience, because my new Alpha would teach me. I don't know why he'd smirked when he said it, but regardless of the reason, I don't have any other options.

I'd signed the contract with a shaking hand.

I stumble as I'm pulled into the white tent. Inside, it is humid. Several large tubs full of steaming water crowd too close together. Most are occupied already. I don't know where to look, so I drop my eyes to the drab carpet beneath my bare feet, feeling my skin heat in a blush. Too many naked bodies, none of them wolves.

A heavy hand hits my back, and I stumble forward, unable to stop myself from looking up as we move farther inside. This time, I see the iron collars and long lengths of chain, and my blush dies, replaced by a sense of dizziness that only grows stronger when a blue-skinned woman marches my way.

"Christ, Ronan! Where are his bindings?" she snaps over my shoulder, crossing two of her six arms over her ample chest. A third grips me tightly, digging into the bruises Ronan left.

"He's a volunteer," Ronan says. His voice is like birdsong.

"A volunteer?" She glares down at me, her lips pursed. "Haven't had one of those in a while. Go along then." She waves him away with a fourth hand before tugging me toward an empty tub.

She yanks my shirt over my head, catching a few strands of my hair with the motion. "In you get, you poor fool."

I want to ask why I'm a fool, but I can't find my voice, so instead I clamber over the edge of the tub and into the hot water. It feels nice on my chilled skin. Even though I'd washed the turkey blood and feathers off in a stream while I waited for Beta, I still feel dirty.

I can't help but wonder how much of that blood belonged to Alpha.

At the thought, I scrub my skin harder, the harsh soap leaving it red. Then, I duck under the water to wash and rinse my hair. The blue lady doesn't let me linger, snapping her fingers impatiently before I finish.

"Well, hurry up, then. There are others waiting," she says. "Besides, we have to get you ready. That's a lot of hair to braid." She tugs on the end of it slightly too hard, and I wince before climbing out of the water, shivering. She tosses me a thin towel, nearly threadbare, then drags me out of the tent while I'm still wrapping it around my body. "Come on. Keep up," she snaps over her shoulder as she leads me to another tent.

There, I'm shoved and pinched and powdered until I sneeze as they get me ready for what they keep calling 'the auction'. A pair of Brownies yank on my hair until it's up in a crown braid. My shoulders feel naked, even more so when I realize that the only things that they are giving me to wear are several lengths of gold chains to drape around my neck and a pair of tight gold shorts that cover less than a pair of boxers. They fit snug around my ass and cock.

The women don't listen to my protests, talking over me as they argue about whether to line my eyes or not. They decide against it. I'm still protesting when they prod me out of the tent. The large man is waiting, glaring at a watch on his wrist.

"Did you have to wait for his hair to grow?" He grunts at the women.

"Now, Ronan... If you think you can do better, I'll let you handle the next batch while *I* stand around looking pretty." The blue woman crosses both sets of arms and lifts her eyebrow.

Ronan doesn't answer. He grabs my arm again and pulls me past several rows of pens. At first, I keep my eyes on the ground, trying to avoid the sharpest pieces of gravel. But once I do glance up, I stumble.

There are *people* in the pens…dressed like me, in that they are hardly dressed at all, with heavy shackles around their wrists and collars around their necks. Too many species to count. I recognize some from my studies, like the bean-sidhe. She has a riot of dark hair that falls over her pale shoulders, the ends trailing blood as red as her eyes. A metal, spider-like gag keeps her mouth wired closed.

I shudder and look away, my focus landing on a centaur. Iron chains keep him hobbled. I don't like the way he leers at me as I pass, so I go back to staring at my feet, until Ronan stops and I nearly trip. Ronan keeps his grip on my arm as he slides a gold key into the heavy lock on one of the pens. He opens it the smallest crack, just wide enough he can shove me inside.

The door slams shut behind me, and I cringe. Unlike the other pens, which seem to be sorted by species, there's an eclectic assortment in here. I skirt along the edge toward one who smells familiar.

I don't know him. The wolf isn't from my pack, but it seems better than lingering by the harpy with her clicking beak and piercing gaze. Unfortunately, the male growls as I approach, tucking his chin and baring his teeth. Instinctively I cower, exposing my neck. The submissiveness helps. If only my wolf understood.

After a few seconds, the much larger wolf straightens. "What'd a pretty thing like you do to end up here?" he grunts, voice raspy. His teeth are sharp, betraying his agitation.

I smooth sweaty palms over my thighs to dry them. "My Beta brought me. He said it's where everyone comes to learn how to take care of themselves."

The other wolf stares for a second before letting out a roar of laughter. "And you believed him? What did you do to your Beta, not put out enough?"

I cower further, shoulders hunching. "What are you talking about?"

He shakes his head, still snickering. "This is a Flesh Market, pup. You know, where people come to buy slaves?"

"Slaves?" I yelp, louder than I'd intend. "No, I signed a work contract."

Finally, his laughter dies, but now he is staring at me with pity instead. "For how long? One month? Two?"

I swallow. "Two years."

"Oh, poor pup. Nobody survives two years. They'll chew you up and spit out your bones." He pats my shoulder like he wants to console me, take the sting out of the words that won't stop circling in my ears.

"No, I don't believe you. Beta said it was normal. He said it would—"

"Your Beta lied."

Before I can do more than suck in a breath, the gate to the pen is pulled open, and Ronan steps into the doorway. He points at the harpy, who is dragged out by a pair of men in leather. They lead her up a set of stairs onto what looks like a stage. I recognize the voice that starts speaking as the jinni from the tent, but I can barely make out what he's saying over the buzzing in my ears.

I want to defend Beta, but even when I close my eyes, I can see the pity on the other wolf's face and I know he isn't just being cruel. Beta *had* lied.

It doesn't take long for the pen to slowly empty and soon, only the wolf and I are left. He shakes his head at me when it's his turn. "Good luck, pup. Maybe you'll get lucky and be a bed slave. They last a bit longer."

I have a moment of horror at the thought but then, he is gone.

I am alone.

Not for long.

The gate opens again, and I am waved forward. I stumble out, my heart pounding in my chest. If the other wolf thought his words were comforting, he was wrong.

I don't want to be a bed slave.

I don't want to be a slave at all.

I want to go home to the safety of my bedroom. I should have just run when Beta told me to wait, disappeared into the woods.

The stage is hot when I stumble onto it. I can't see much of the audience behind the bright lights, but I can hear them, muttering already.

The jinni from the tent places a cold hand on my lower back and urges me farther into the light. "I have a special treat for y'all tonight. Not only is it his *first* time to market" — the audience hollers and the jinni has to pause until the sound fades — "but it's his first time for *everything.* He is...completely untouched. A true virgin."

My skin burns, and I whine as he spills my secrets to the world. The crowd hoots again. He fondles my ass in a way that makes me yelp before he abandons me to their hungry eyes.

The jinni keeps speaking, moving over to a podium as he points at people in the audience, but I stop listening, dropping my hands in front of my crotch to hide the obscene bulge my cock makes, even soft. It only makes them yell louder.

The jinni says something then the people in the audience yell back. It takes me too long to realize they are bidding.

On me.

Chapter Five

Master

I don't pay much attention to the wares being brought out. I've had harpy before and have no need to try it again. Kelpie wouldn't be bad, I suppose, but I don't feel like sacrificing my pool for the entirety of the upcoming summer, if he makes it that long. I consider bidding on the other wolf in the lot, just in case, but I refuse to acknowledge the possibility that someone else will take home what I've already decided is mine.

Finally, Niall calls my little wolf onto the stage. He is clearly overwhelmed by the crowd and the lights, his skin pinkening quickly, and it doesn't take long for the bids to start climbing. They increase even faster when the boy drops his hands in front of his crotch in embarrassment. It makes his innocence even more obvious.

I wonder how it will taste on him.

Clearly, I'm not the only one imagining his sweetness. Immediately, an Ankhuban on the other side of the audience hollers out a bid nearly twice as high as the current one. I recognize him, even if I can't think of his name. He runs a brothel in Zades, and though it's been a few years since I've partaken in its many pleasures, I remember enough to know that the little wolf would do well there—at least, until one of the clients eats him.

Most of the other bidders drop out quickly. He is too small to work the giants' forges in Oppenhelm and too big for the pixies' sweatshops. At the current bid, he'd cost more than he could ever produce.

Still, the thought of the Ankhuban outbidding me is annoying, so I raise the bid again.

If *anyone* eats the little wolf, it's going to be me.

Soon, it is just me and the Ankhuban, calling out our bids in rapid fire. I growl as the Ankhuban outbids me again, tiring of the game. I shout out an astronomically high number, enough to buy me a helicopter...if I didn't have one already.

The Ankhuban grimaces, twisting his face like he swallowed a lemon, but he doesn't counter.

The jinni pauses, waiting for other takers, before banging his gavel. "Sold!"

I want to storm up to the stage and drag the little wolf right off, sink my fangs into his flesh and suck him dry until every ounce of his essence lives on beneath my skin, but I restrain myself. With as much as I've just spent on him, I know I need to keep him around for a few feedings at least, if only to keep Maggie off my back.

Besides, even if the BAA doesn't catch wind of it—which they would, because Niall runs a legal, if socially distasteful, business—I'd just have to go shopping again in a few days.

I only half listen to Niall's spiel about where to pick up our new merchandise. I know the drill. I go over to meet Niall at the Bursar's tent and make the payment arrangements, then scrawl my name in spelled ink at the bottom of the contract.

The Binding snaps into place. It is barely more than a flutter against my skin. It amuses me to imagine the little wolf's reaction, the small yelp of surprise I bet that he's making right at this moment. The Binding takes the form of a gold collar, branded with a mark of ownership. *My* mark. If the contract is broken, either by the little wolf trying to run or my unlikely death, the mark will vanish, and he will be immediately returned to the Flesh Market, either for me to reclaim or for him to find a new placement until his contract is up.

I can't wait to see him in my collar.

Niall snags the contract and rolls it up, slipping it into a safe behind him and locking it quickly. "I hope you enjoy your purchase, and thank you for shopping with us. See you in a few weeks." He winks before waving me out. This time, as I leave, I reach out and grab the gold tassel, yanking it free. I laugh as the side of the tent unfurls with a snap and Niall curses.

I ignore his hollering as I stroll toward the other end of the lot. Unlike the stage, which is gussied up to look its best, pickup is little more than chain link and cement. I flash my signet ring at one of the handlers.

"Are you taking him with you or would you like transport?" the handler asks in a bored voice.

"Transport," I answer immediately, as I always do. My way of traveling is convenient and quick but not conducive to passengers. Besides, it'll give me time to make sure my new pet's quarters are prepared. I haven't had a wolf in a few years, so I'll need to have my servants clean out the silver pen. I make a mental note to have them check the perimeter fence as well, since a wolf will need space to run on the full moon, and I don't want any surprises next month.

The last thing I feel like doing is chasing a mutt around the countryside like a fool.

"That'll cost extra." The handler's pen hovers over his paperwork as he waits for verification.

I wave him off. "Not an issue." A glance at my watch makes me grimace. "Have him sent to my estate in Brekkan.

"Yes, sir. It'll be a two-day trip…unless you want overnight delivery?"

I consider it. "That'll get him there tomorrow?"

"Late evening, most likely."

"Go for it. I'll pay the premium." I grin as I glance at my watch. "Get him there in time for supper and I'll double your tip."

The handler gives his first real grin. "Yes, sir."

* * * *

It's early afternoon the next day when a heavy knocking sounds on the front door of my manor. Even with my advanced hearing, I can barely hear it from my armchair upstairs in the library. Unlike my old castle, this manor is far better insulated, both from the elements and stray noise. Modern plumbing and a working heating system won me over a several centuries ago. I'm still not used to windows with glass instead of shutters.

I give Lucifer one last pet before I set the purring cat on the floor and stand. Except for the pair of servants who'd just finished cleaning the pen in the basement — who should be making their way out through one of the side entrances any moment — the estate is empty. I prefer to spend the first few days with a new feeder alone.

Well, except for Maggie...but she hardly counts.

I'm a possessive bastard. I learned my lesson a long time ago, and servants willing to work for my kind are rare enough, without rumors of them becoming dessert spreading around.

The knock echoes a second time. "Hold your kelpies, I'm coming," I holler as I take the last few steps to the main floor two at a time. *They made good time.* It's only three, hours earlier than I expected.

I yank open the door and immediately look past the handler holding a clipboard out for a signature. It isn't hard to spot the wooden crate strapped to a dolly behind him. A large black arrow points to the sky, over the words 'This Side Up'. A young elf with acne leans on the dolly handle, chewing gum while he waits.

I scrawl my signature at the bottom of the paperwork without looking. "Bring him inside. I've got his pen set up in the basement."

The handler shrugs, popping his gum before he waves the other two men up the stairs in front of him to help with the crate. I back inside and step out of the way, pointing them toward the door to the cellar stairs. Two of the handlers stop at the top and confer between each other while bubblegum guy plays on his phone.

It takes only a second for their incompetence to irk me, and I strongly consider telling them to leave it and let me do it myself. Finally, though, the taller of the two men grabs the handle of the dolly and spins it around, backing down the cellar stairs with it while the other grabs the crate to help guide.

I hear a cry from inside as the dolly drops down the first step. I listen harder, just in case the little wolf injured himself in surprise but hear nothing else as they slowly make their way down. I don't smell any blood, so I don't stop them.

I can't trust the little wolf not to shift and get snappy or I'd let him out up here. Not that he is any threat to me... It'd take a lot more than a few bite marks to prove a danger, but I hate the idea of having to punish my new pet already.

I want him to *earn* his first punishment. They always do, eventually. Sometimes it takes a few days, maybe a week, but eventually, my pets always test the limits I set. It's just a matter of *which* rule they break that determines the harshness of the reprimand.

I like a bit of backtalk, even a few scratches. I don't mind a feeder with the right amount of fight to stir up my predator drive. But I won't abide theft or violence against my servants.

I follow the handlers down into the basement and gesture to the silver pen. The bars go from floor to ceiling, just enough space between each one that I could slip a wrist through but not an elbow. Eight feet by eight, there is enough room for the twin-size mattress to fit in the center with room left over for a curtained-off shower and toilet.

I wonder how long he'll have to stay down here. I haven't bought the contract of a volunteer in ages, and it had only been for a two-week gig. The criminals always cause problems—stealing, attacking the servants, trying to run despite the consequences. Most never make it upstairs.

Chapter Six

Pet

The wooden box I've been shoved into smells like vomit.

Which makes sense, since I've thrown up twice already. I tried staying standing, but my knees could only hold me up so long. There isn't enough room for me to fully sit, but my knees scraped against the side. I've had to half-crouch instead, and the position is killing my calves. I can't feel my toes. When I try to straighten, the box shifts, and I lose my footing. Sometime after that, my legs cramp painfully, the feeling worsening when I can't force them straight.

It's a good thing I'm not claustrophobic, just motion sick.

Abruptly, the whole world lurches, and I cry out, the first sound I've let myself make. The crate is suspended in midair for an eternity before it lands on something hard with a thump. My elbow collides with the plywood, and I know I'll have a bruise later. There's too little room for me to twist my other arm around to rub the pain away. All I manage is to smash my fingers when the crate lurches again, then again.

I think I'm going down a flight of stairs.

I give up trying to count them after the fourth, since there's little point in knowing how many stairs I'd need to climb to get out if I can't even guess what state I'm in. All I know is that I was in this box for what had to be hours before the rumbling of an engine lulled me to sleep, and we were still driving when I woke up.

The jolting motion makes me queasy again, but each eternity-long fall down to the next step racks the panic up further as I wait, breathless, for whoever's carting me around like luggage to make a mistake and send me tumbling.

Instead, there's a final drop then the ride smooths out, which helps my nausea a little, until we stop. I smash face-first into the plywood as the crate tips forward to stand upright again.

Nothing happens for several minutes. I crane my ears to hear outside. A loud wrenching screech pierces my ears, and I slap my hands over them with a whimper. Light creeps in from each of the seams as the side of the crate is slowly pried away from the rest. The edge of what looks like a crowbar slips between the two pieces of wood to crank it farther open.

I instinctively clench my eyes shut against the growing light. It's not the burning brightness of the noon sun or even the gentle lullaby of Goddess Moon, but after so long in the crate, the artificial light is painfully bright.

"Come out, come out, little wolf," a deep voice singsongs. It sounds amused, and I find myself torn. As much as I want out of the vomit-soaked crate, at least in here I'm safe. Slowly, I open my eyes a slit and look out.

The box is sitting off-center in a large silver dog kennel. It's probably the same size as my bedroom at the pack house, with a bare mattress in the center of the cement floor. On the other side, farthest from the stairs, an opaque vinyl shower curtain dangles. There's nothing else to see, so I finally look at the man leaning against the silver bars.

It's the same man, the one from the jinni's tent...the one from the auction.

Levi... That's what the jinni called him. He is wearing a black button-down open at the throat, his long inky hair pulled into a braid. My cheeks burn when I realize I'm just as overwhelmed by his commanding aura now as I was before, back in that tent with Beta. It feels stronger here. I fight the urge to crawl out on my hands and knees and prostrate myself at his feet.

Why did I never feel this urge with Alpha? Even the wolf in my belly cowers.

Something on my face must give me away because he smirks. "Come now, little wolf. Out you get. You know you want to."

I whimper at the order. Is it this collar that makes me want to obey, some magic in the binding? Or is it me? Slowly, I unfold myself, my knees screaming. I crawl out onto the cement directly outside the crate, unwilling to move closer.

"Don't be scared, boy. Come here." He snaps his fingers.

I can't help but get offended. "I'm not a dog," I whisper, face twisting in a scowl as I wish my voice was louder.

Levi just laughs. "Of course you're not, little wolf. Now be a good boy and come on over." This time, he pats his leg.

"I'm not a *dog*," I repeat, louder this time. It doesn't stop me from gripping the side of the crate and dragging myself up onto my feet to limp toward him.

"You're a cute one, though a bit of a mess. Go ahead and turn around for me." He twirls his index finger in a circle and eyes me critically, ignoring my protest. Slowly, hesitantly, I obey, wishing I was dressed in something...more. Just more. These tight shorts hide nothing.

"At least transit didn't bang you up too badly. There's a shower over there." He gestures toward the curtain. "Get cleaned up. Don't bother putting these back on. You won't need them." He pinches the fabric of the shorts between his thumb and forefinger, catching the skin of my ass. He laughs at my yelp before adding, "I'll be back for dinner in an hour."

Just the word *dinner* makes my stomach growl. I haven't eaten real food since my shift nearly five days ago, when I'd gorged on whatever creatures my wolf had hunted, but the calories have already burned away by the change back to human.

I don't know what he'll bring with him, and I find that I don't care, as long as it's edible.

Levi straightens up and slips out of the pen, closing the gate behind him. He spends a second with a heavy-duty lock, then starts for the stairs, whistling as he goes up them. I don't know what to think about my new...quarters. If I ignore the fact that it's made up of bars instead of walls and that the mattress sits right on the floor instead of a frame, it's not too bad.

It stirs up memories of being a pup, the few days after my first shift when my mother was only crating me instead of trying to drown me.

Peering around the curtain reveals a steel shower head and a drain. There's a small shelf screwed to one of the bars, with a bottle of two-in-one shampoo and conditioner and a smaller bottle of body wash, and that's it. There's no washcloth or towel.

Better to be cold and clean than covered in vomit, I guess. I spin on the water and give it several minutes to warm up. Testing it on the back of my hand periodically proves that it goes from icy to merely cold, so I decide that's the best I'm going to get.

Trying to strip out of the shorts makes me fear they've decided to meld with my body. Between the sweat and vomit, they're glued to my bony hips. I have to peel them away, wincing as they tug on my skin like wallpaper off drywall. I toss them over by the crate.

The frigid water sprouts goosebumps on my flesh as soon as I step under it. Shivering, I wash up as fast as I can, spinning the knob quicker than I ever have in my life. Even the scant few minutes I was under leaves me with pins and needles. Wringing out my long hair sends a fresh cascade of iciness over my shoulder and chest.

Not for the first time in my life, I wish I had control over my shift. Fur would be warmer than flesh right now. There aren't any blankets on the mattress to steal, either, and no other clothing to change into. I briefly try using the curtain to dry off, but the vinyl doesn't do anything but smear the beads of water around my skin. I give up.

Instead, I crouch down by the mattress and wrap my arms around my legs. I can't lean against the bars — my skin is already starting to itch from the proximity to the silver—but I don't want to get the bed wet, either. I refuse to go any closer than necessary to the crate. It still reeks of vomit.

I don't hear the door at the top of the stairs open. I just know it must have, because I hear footsteps coming down. I sit up onto my knees, not even caring that it leaves me horribly exposed. I'm starving, and if looking agreeable gets me food faster, I'll do it.

Levi had changed at some point. Instead of a suit, he's in a pair of black lounge pants and nothing else. His chest is pale but not sickly—like a marble statue. From his broad shoulders to his tight pecs, his abs down to the V of his hips, I can find nothing to criticize.

Nothing except his hands.

They're empty.

"I thought you said you were coming back with dinner?" I say without thinking about the consequences of speaking without permission.

"*For* dinner," Levi corrects, twisting his mouth up in a sharp smile.

I don't understand what he means, until he steps, barefoot, into the pen and looms over me. His smile widens, revealing four sharp white fangs. I drop back on my ass, ignoring the frigid cement on my skin as I scuttle backward until my back hits the silver bars, then I scream.

It feels like that time I grabbed a hot pan without thinking. I jerk away, but that brings me closer to Levi and his teeth.

"There's nowhere to go, so you might as well relax," Levi coaxes as he stalks closer. "I'm told it only hurts the first time."

"I'll be good. You don't have to do this. I'm a hard worker, or...or I will be, when you tell me what you want me to do," I babble, cringing away as far as I can without touching the silver a second time. "Just tell me what to do."

"Don't worry, little wolf. You don't have to do anything." Levi gives a dangerous grin then he is on me, his fangs clamping down on my throat, piercing like daggers through my skin.

My breath catches as I try to scream, but no sound comes out. At first, it only burns. Soon, though, more than pain fills me. It's fear — a wild, swirling panic from both me and my wolf.

The jaws around my throat demand submission, and my whole body goes limp.

The agony spikes as the man— "*Alpha*", my wolf growls, the most lucid I've felt him in ages — groans, yanking me closer, his fangs shifting under my flesh. But then it fades, my eyes growing blurry. My hands, which had been curled into useless little fists against his skin, go lax.

"Please," I try to plead, struggling to push him off with no luck. I'm not ready to die, but I'm not strong enough to save myself.

Weak, that's what I am. My mother knew it, my pack knew it and now, my Alpha knows as well. Tears spill down my cheeks, and I grow dizzy before slipping into darkness.

Chapter Seven

Master

The little wolf tastes like moonlight. I won't lie and claim he's the best I've ever had. That honor will likely always go to a phoenix I'd stumbled on back in what used to be Tampa, mid-twentieth century. Still, he's delicious, and I groan, pulling his struggling body closer. He's not strong enough to push me off, so I ignore his hands when they try to shove at my chest. My feeders always fight the first few times.

If he survives the next few weeks, I'll consider teaching him passivity. For now, the struggle is exciting, each whimper fluttering against my skin like moth wings.

I'm not worried about drinking too deeply. I'm confident from past experiences that his wolf won't allow it. I'll get a mouthful of fur before he's in any danger, so I let myself get lost in his taste, in the feel of his smaller body held tight to mine.

He finally submits, dropping his hands away from my skin, his neck opening further. It's not until I notice that each swallow brings me less blood that I realize… *He hasn't submitted, he's passed out.*

I tear my fangs from his throat with a curse, dragging him over to the mattress. At least the coagulating agent in my saliva has clotted the wound, preventing any further blood loss, but his skin, which had already been pale, is nearing gray, his cheeks sunken.

He looks so much smaller on the mattress, his body limp. *And younger, too. Too young to die because of carelessness.* I don't know why his wolf didn't surface. It should have, despite the silver. I don't choose wolves often, but he's not the first I've held here, and it hadn't bothered the others.

He is smaller, though. Perhaps his wolf is weak.

Whatever the reason, it's too late to fix my mistake. I can only decide where to go from here. I can't un-drink, but I can make him more comfortable. I scoop him back up off the mattress as I come to a decision. If he can't, or won't, shift — not even to save himself — he's no danger to the staff. If he dies, it should be somewhere warm.

I carry him upstairs to the small room off the kitchen, the one my feeders typically work for months to earn, if they earn it at all, and set him on the narrow bed. A small twinge of guilt tugs at my chest as I cover him with the pale blue comforter.

I don't like this feeling. It rides sour in my stomach. It's rare that I make mistakes — or at least, mistakes that I care about. He wouldn't be the first or second or even tenth feeder I've lost, but it feels different.

I can't resist the sudden urge to touch him. His hair is soft under my fingers as I brush it away from his face, then smooth my fingertips over his unmarked forehead. Is it because, unlike the others I've taken, he's not a criminal? Or is it his age, only nineteen with an entire life to live?

It makes me wonder why he signed the contract. A Flesh Market is the last resort, the place someone goes when they are out of options.

Who took this pretty boy's options away?

Staring at him gets me no answers, but I'm afraid to leave. He doesn't deserve to die alone. So, against my nature, I sit on the bed and carefully shift his head into my lap, humming a song I hadn't thought of in millennia, not since my childhood.

By some miracle, he survives the night.

He doesn't wake up, not even when one of my servants peeks inside. He's only been in my employ for a handful of years, so he stammers as he asks if I need anything. I send him away with a wave of my hand and go back to watching the sleeping wolf in my lap.

The next doesn't leave so easily.

A matronly woman, Maggie has been with me the longest, nearly four decades in my employ under her belt. She was young when she joined my staff, sent over from the employment agency to cover for a no call, no show. She'd told me, "Just one more day, Mister Levi," for the first two years she worked for me.

She still says it sometimes, when I do something particularly stubborn.

She's in her sixties now, her red hair streaked with white. Though age has tamed her fiery locks, it hasn't tamed her mouth. "Master Levi, you should be ashamed. Did you bother to feed the poor boy before you turned him into a snack? Look at him. He's skin and bones." She tuts. "Poor thing."

I don't have time to answer before she spins on her heel and leaves. I hear metal banging from the kitchen. That, combined with the curses and muttering, make it clear she's not happy. I go to sit up but the little wolf in my lap whines. His fingers clench my black satin sleep pants.

"Don't you dare get out of that bed, Mister, or I'll change all your passwords," she hollers, and I cringe back into the bed. There are days I can barely figure out how to turn the fancy holo-top on without her, let alone muddle through *that*.

"Yes, ma'am." A small part of me wants to get up just in spite, since taking orders — from a human, no less — grates a bit, but a larger part decides to enjoy the feeling of the boy in my lap.

He starts to stir as Maggie hustles back into the room, a bowl of soup and a large piece of bread balanced in her hands. "Go ahead and sit him up. My chicken noodle soup hasn't failed to wake up hungry bellies yet."

I shift higher on the bed, bringing the little wolf with me. His head lolls on his neck until I shift his back to my chest. "Come on, Pet. Time to wake up."

Maggie waves the bowl in front of Eryn, the steam hitting his face then mine. I wrinkle my nose at the smell of dead flesh, but it seems Eryn isn't opposed. The little wolf whimpers again, turning his face to follow the scent, even before his eyes open.

I can tell when he wakes up because he freezes, then cringes away from Maggie like she's holding a gun instead of a bowl of soup. "Hush, Pet," I murmur, stroking what I hope is calming circles against his chest.

"Don't call me that," Eryn snaps, though his voice is more rasp than anything. It's cute, so I just smile.

"Maggie brought you something to eat." Hesitant to spook him, I keep one hand plastered to his belly, which, as Maggie pointed out, is far too thin, reaching for the bowl with the other. "Let me help you."

"My throat hurts."

I feel the urge to apologize but swallow it down. "It'll get better. Soup will help."

"Too tired." He sounds it, too. But he needs to eat before he sleeps again, or he'll never recover his strength.

"Just a few bites. Here." I balance the bowl on my knee and carefully spoon out a bite, holding it up to Eryn's mouth. "Be a good boy."

He hesitates before he opens his mouth, allowing me to slip the spoon between his lips. They're full, plump—begging me to suck one into my mouth, but I don't fuck my feeders—not unless they ask, anyway, which hasn't happened since my last trip to Old York, however long ago that was. Then again, none of my previous feeders have been quite like Eryn.

"How is it?" I ask, genuinely curious. I don't usually wonder about mortal food, but from the little moan that slips out of Eryn's mouth, I can't help it.

"It's good," he mumbles, his eyes following the spoon back to the bowl.

"Don't worry. There's plenty more," Maggie says, and I nearly tip the bowl. I'd forgotten she was standing in the doorway. "Just holler when you're ready, boys."

Eryn stiffens as she leaves. I set the spoon down to rub more circles on his belly until he calms, though it makes me even more aware of his state of undress. A few inches lower and I could take him in hand, stroke him to hardness and coax him to spill for me.

"No need to fret, little wolf. I won't need to eat for a few more weeks," I soothe. It's not strictly true. I would prefer to eat more often, but for some reason, I hate the thought of him worrying over it. Instead of relaxing him, though, it only makes him stiffen further. "Come now. It won't be like this next time, I promise." I take the spoon again and ladle up another bit of soup, holding it out. He hesitates, but just as I'm about to give up, he leans forward, closing his lips around the spoon.

I've never wanted to be a piece of cutlery more.

Silently, he finishes the bowl of soup but declines the bread. "Throat still hurts," he finally answers in reply to my attempt at coaxing.

"Okay. We'll try that later." I drop the bread into the bowl and set it aside.

"So, um…" Eryn shifts in my lap, like he wants to pull away but doesn't want to offend me.

Gently, I tip him off my lap onto the bed, taking a second to inspect the deep bruise on his neck with a frown. It should have healed by now. Wolves are well known for their speedy recovery.

"Levi?" His voice shakes me from my thought.

"Call me 'Master'," I correct immediately. Good habits are easier to teach than bad habits are to break.

His skin turns a pretty pink. "Um, Master, is this…going to be my only job?" He lifts his fingers to the bruise, his eyes meeting mine for a second. They are big and blue. I could drown in them.

"Yes, little wolf. This is going to be your only job." I smile, reaching out to card my fingers through his hair. He flinches away and, for some reason, that hurts. It'll be okay. He'll get used to it. They always do.

Chapter Eight

Pet

I don't see anyone but Maggie for three weeks. She brings me breakfast in the morning and dinner in the evenings. Sometimes, she stays for a few minutes to chat, telling me little things, like about the weather outside or what one of her nephews did that was so funny.

I find myself waiting for her visits like an addict.

This room is less itchy than the silver pen and warmer, but it's just as barren. The mattress has sheets, there's a nightstand with a little lamp and an actual toilet and shower in the attached bathroom, but that's it. There's nothing to do but sit and wait. I've taken to counting the carpet threading. At least it's warm.

I'm going crazy in here.

It doesn't help that I can feel Goddess Moon bloating each night. I can't see her—there isn't even a window to stare out of—but I don't need to. It's days away from full, and I have no idea what I'll do—no idea if I'll manage to shift.

I drag my pillow off the mattress and drop it onto the ground, then collapse down onto my stomach. It must be dinner time by now. It has been forever since lunch. Maggie never stays very long at dinner time, as she says she has to get food ready for the entire staff, but I'll take a few seconds of time with a real person over nothing.

If I run my hand over the carpet to the left, I find the color looks darker, so I start running my hand over different spots until I have a very juvenile picture of a smiley face on the carpet. I fight the urge to give it a name.

"Well, don't you look cute?"

I scramble to my feet at the unexpected voice, too deep to be Maggie's. I drag the pillow with me and hold it in front of my hips, hoping it will provide at least a semblance of modesty. Levi is standing in the doorway, leaning against the doorframe with a smirk.

"Sorry, Master." The words spill out of my lips immediately, even though I'm not sure what I'm sorry for. Not realizing he was there? Not greeting him immediately? "Is it…um? Time for another…?" I brush over the side of my neck as my heart beats quicker.

I'm answered with a long stretch of silence. Levi's face is a blank mask, but eventually, it softens. He holds out his hand. "Would you like to go for a walk first?"

"Yes, please." I rush to his side, the desire to get out of this room drowning out my fear. His hand is twice the size of mine but colder. He gives me a tug, leading me through into a kitchen.

Everything is iridescent—top-of-the-line appliances equipped for solar charging, pearly countertops, pale cabinets. Maggie is missing, but a steaming pot of something that smells delicious proves she'll be back. Before she does, Master opens the far door and pulls me through, into the back yard.

It's not quite dark yet, the sun hovering near the tops of the trees at the far edge of the yard. It's chilly, especially given my lack of dress, but I barely notice. I suck in deep breaths of the fresh air, hurrying down into the grass. It prickles against my feet, the dirt damp. Now it's my turn to tug Master Levi behind me.

He laughs but allows it. "It's strange, Pet. I find myself overcome with the desire to apologize for not letting you out sooner," he says, and though he sounds amused, I can hear confusion hiding faintly beneath it. "I didn't want to hamper your recovery, but perhaps I misjudged."

I stumble at the reminder that he nearly killed me. I'd managed to, not *forget* exactly, but ignore the memory of his fangs piercing my flesh—the way no amount of struggling could push him off me, the pain and not even being able to speak.

"Hey, take a breath now."

I don't realize I've stopped breathing, standing frozen, until he shakes me. Sucking in a breath makes me dizzy, but I do it anyway, then another.

"I want to sit down," I manage to squeeze out of my tight throat. He pushes me gently toward a stone bench. Shivering at the chill, I perch on the edge. Wrapping my arms around myself, I whisper, "The other wolf in the cage said I wouldn't survive this contract. He…he was right, wasn't he?"

Master Levi doesn't answer, which is an answer on its own. He just crouches in front of me.

"It's okay," I say quickly, but I know I'm consoling myself. "It's okay." I bury my face in my hands to block out the view of the yard I won't ever get to run through and the man who will likely kill me.

"Why *did* you sign that contract?" Master Levi finally asks. He grips my wrists as he pulls them back from my face, forcing me to meet his dark gold eyes. They swim with curiosity.

I shrug and look away. "I don't have anywhere else to go. Beta said... It doesn't matter, does it? I'm here, and you're going to kill me."

"I don't think I want you to die," Master Levi says it softly, and his voice is odd, like the words are just as much of a surprise to him as they are to me. "I promise to try to stay in control."

"Okay," I agree, knowing it won't matter. Promises are meant to be broken, and sooner or later, he'll tire of me, just like everyone else has. I jerk to my feet and pointedly look away. "Can we walk now?"

"Sure." He stands as well. He doesn't take my hand this time, just trails behind me, letting me set the pace. I pay little attention to the garden, my mood soured. I might as well have stayed in my room.

I stop abruptly. "Can you just bite me and get it over with?"

"If that's what you want," Master Levi says calmly, closer behind me than I thought.

"I do." I clench my fists at my sides. The waiting is the worst part. I expect him to lunge again but instead, a gentle finger strokes over my shoulder, slow and soft. It sends a shiver through me, and heat floods my cheeks.

He moves my hair away from my neck, carefully draping it over my other shoulder. My body goes stiffer than the marble statue beside me when he presses his lips against the side of my neck, dancing over my pulse point as I wait for the pain.

It doesn't come.

Instead, he slides his tongue over my skin, slipping over my neck and up to a spot right under my ear that sends electricity through my whole body. I shudder, my neck opening to him as a gasp escapes my lips. He curves his lips up as he works that spot.

My dick stiffens. If it gets any harder, I'll be able to tell the time from its shadow. It's confusing, the fear of being bitten mixing with the arousal. I don't know whether to pull away or press into him.

Maybe he senses my uncertainty, because he curls his arm around my waist, pulling me against his body as he sucks on my neck. His erection is large and commandeers all my attention like a blinking arrow where it presses into my lower back. I rock against it and this time, it's his turn to groan.

His mouth pops off my neck and his breath tickles my ear. "Such a good boy. Do you want me to make you feel good?" He flattens his hand on my stomach, sliding down toward my hips. It stops just inches above where I want it, where I *need* it. No one has ever touched me like that, though I've dreamed of it at night.

I shouldn't want it. Not here, not now. Not with him. My body doesn't listen.

I whimper, hips thrusting out as I try to get closer to his hand, but he doesn't let me, pinning me in place against him. "Use your words, little wolf. Can I make you feel good?"

"Yes," I gasp out, nearly in tears. "Please. I've never... It's never felt like this." *Never felt like I'm going to die if someone doesn't touch me.* Instinctively, I know better than to reach for it myself.

If he answers, I don't hear it, because he curls his large hand around my dick, and I'm lost to the feeling. It's like fireworks exploding in my body. I can't help the way my hips thrust up, fucking into his palm.

He chuckles but it's playful and warm. "There you go. That's a good boy. Make yourself feel good."

His permission helps me let go, and soon, my whole weight is resting against his chest, my body held up only by his arms as all my attention is on the orgasm spiking in my groin, climbing higher than it's ever been before.

Even my inner wolf isn't fighting it.

I barely notice the bite of pain at the crook of my neck, just a shadow behind the blinding pleasure. He tightens his hand before giving a little twist just below the sensitive head and it's enough to tip me over the edge. I cry out as I spill, pumping seed from my dick to fertilize the grass.

It's only as my body goes boneless that I feel the fangs pulling out of my flesh, barely giving me time to be afraid before they are gone. He laps his tongue over the newly opened wounds, but it only hurts for a second. I shiver at the mix of pain and pleasure.

"Is…?" I clear my throat. "Will it be like that every time now?"

"If you'd like. I certainly enjoyed it." He lets go of my dick, lifting his hand up in front of me, cum glistening on his fingers. He shifts me slightly so he can suck them into his mouth. He cleans each one slowly. "You taste delicious." My skin grows hot as I watch, and he grins. "Such a pretty blush."

If I was pink before, I must be beet red now. My gaze drops, locking on the monster tenting his trousers. "You're still hard." Will he want me to take care of him next? Do I want to? I realize that I do, though I'm afraid of disappointing him. The only dick I've ever touched is my own, and it is nothing like the size of his. Will it feel the same in my hand? Will he like the same things?

"Yes," he says, but that's it. He doesn't pressure me to fix it, which makes me want to please him even more. It is a strange feeling — one I don't understand. I shouldn't want this man to touch me when I know someday his touch will be the one that kills me. Shouldn't want to bring him the same pleasure he gave me.

"Can I help?"

Chapter Nine

Master

"Can I help?" Eryn asks, his face so hopeful I know I couldn't deny him, even if I wanted to.

"Would you like to?" I ask instead of answering, not willing to push the little wolf too far. I'm certain the rough first feeding has traumatized him, and while this one has gone better, I don't want to risk the progress we've made.

He bites his lip. It makes me want to sink my teeth into its fullness. I don't, not this time, but the thought makes my dick throb harder. I want to suck the little rubies from it, then steal every breath from his mouth.

Eryn nods slowly, his focus locked below my waist.

I let him go carefully, then gesture to the grass. "On your knees, little wolf. I'll give you what you need."

He drops so quickly to his knees that I think for a second he's fallen. I can't resist petting my hand through his hair before I open my pants and take my dick in hand.

I know I'm large. I don't need to see the way his eyes widen to feel confident in my size, though his surprise makes me grin. His wide eyes only highlight his inexperience. The thought that my dick is the first one he's touched fills me with both pride and a strange sense of possession.

He is *mine.*

I use the hand not holding my dick to keep his head in place. He whimpers, the sound like music in the still air. "Today, just watch," I say, stroking myself slowly in front of him, a tease that quickly has pearly liquid leaking from my slit. I drag my thumb over it in a circle, gathering it up and using it as lube to jack myself.

It doesn't take long, as I'm already on edge from watching the pretty boy come in my arms. "Open your mouth, little wolf. Daddy's made a treat for you." I groan, the words coming out without warning or forethought. Later, I'll regret them. I can't now, not when he's obediently waiting, sticking his tongue out, my cum spilling between his lips and over his chin.

He coughs when one spurt hits his throat but doesn't back away, and it fills me with an unreasonable pride. "*Such* a good boy." I grunt, my hand flying over my dick, working the last few drops out. "Such a *good* boy."

I haven't thought of myself as a *Daddy* in years, not since my last boy betrayed me, literally stabbing me in the back before stealing my prized possession, my *Focus.* The only thing that let me harness the raw magic in my body into the structure of a spell. Barely a decade hadn't been enough to chill my anger at Puck's treachery.

Now isn't the time to give in to these urges, not with a boy who isn't here by choice...not with a boy who doesn't even know what a 'Daddy' is. I need to shove these thoughts back where they came from, bury them like they've been buried for years.

He's my feeder, and that's all.

That's all I can afford for him to be.

I step back and coldly tuck my dick away, doing up my pants. "Time to go back inside." I look pointedly at my watch. I have nowhere better to be, but I can't watch the disappointment flood his face.

He follows me inside like a kicked puppy, silent as I shut him back in his room. I remind myself that I've allowed him upstairs much sooner than any of the others, so my guilt is baseless.

"Maggie will bring you dinner," I say just before I step out, in an attempt to ease the feeling.

It doesn't help, not when I hear the quiet, barely muffled sob as the door latches shut behind me. I force myself to walk away from the room before I can cave to my primal urges. I want to hold him, keep him safe and warm, make him feel good over and over again before dirtying him up.

Instead, I go to my study and drop in front of my computer. I'm done with most of my research and should be in the writing stage, but lately, I haven't felt like threading together the meandering strands of my latest manuscript. I tap my fingers on the keys but don't type anything. I'm still sitting there, staring at the same blank space, when my phone rings an hour later.

At this point, I'll take any distraction, so I don't bother to look at the caller ID before I answer. "Levi."

"It's Aries." My old friend's voice sounds stressed as he speaks. It's been a while since we've spoken—him busy with his new job, me busy with my research. "I've been asked to bring you in on a case."

"That doesn't sound like fun." Spinning my chair to face the window helps me focus on his voice.

"You know the rules."

Unfortunately, I do. I'd only gotten permission to establish permanent residency without the need for periodic check-ins by agreeing to consult as needed for the BAA. Not my idea of a good time, but it was worth it to avoid strangers tramping through my house searching for contraband every few decades.

"What's the case?"

"Classified. Can't say over the phone. I'll text you some coordinates, and we'll make sure an agent is there to transport you to the final location." Aries goes quiet for a few seconds before adding, "Bring your kit."

Well...*that* makes this even more interesting. I sit forward, excitement swirling under my skin. "Been a few years since I've needed that."

"Well, hopefully you're not out of practice." Aries hangs up without waiting for a reply, knowing me well enough to know curiosity will drag me there faster than an explanation.

I stand and shove my chair toward my desk without looking. My kit is locked in the safe behind the abstract painting on the wall, so I take the painting off its hook and set it aside. Keying the security code into the pin pad activates the biometric scanner, but then the door audibly unlocks. Tugging the handle, I swing the door open to stare inside.

I understand why comic book villains rub their hands together. My kit is exactly where I left it, a black duffel bag stuffed with everything I could need to take down an enemy, from saltwater to iron stakes to silver bullets. The Bureau prefers me to use mundane means as much as possible. Using my true form causes problems of its own for Blanks. Apparently, non-magical persons confronted with a Bloodwraith tend to panic, and sometimes that leads to silly things, like jumping off bridges or forgetting to breathe.

Like it's somehow *my* fault that the bloody aura is so intense.

Hence the Dragonsteel dagger I strap to my thigh after changing into my leathers, and the Griffinbone arrows in my quiver on my shoulder.

It's more fun this way, anyway. I love the feel of stretching my muscles, both physically and mentally, to take out an opponent. In the Old Days, it was too easy. No thought, no effort, just Swarm and the problem is solved.

I'm half out of the door when a glance at the darkening sky makes me curse, and I turn around, searching out Maggie. I find her at the small table in the corner of the kitchen, planning out meals for next week.

"I got called out," I say from the doorway. "I need you to have some of the boys bring the wolf downstairs."

Maggie's face twists. "Is that necessary? He's been good."

"It's not a punishment, but I don't know how long I'll be gone. If I'm not back before the full moon, he'll need a safe place to shift. I don't want him on the grounds alone."

I'm hoping to be back in time, since being inside for the full moon will surely be stressful for the little wolf, but working for the bureau never comes with any certainties. I could be home this evening or it could be a week.

She gives a reluctant nod. "Okay, but...try to come back soon."

Chapter Ten

Master

I'm not going to be home soon.

I land on the outskirts of Old York City a few minutes after dawn, then a uniformed BAA officer leads me into Central Park. I'm in my leather jacket and dark jeans, only the badge on a silver chain around my neck proving my affiliation. Tourists point as we pass, snapping pictures, but the natives ignore us. The city is so packed with crime that it's a common occurrence to see the BAA.

The clearing I'm led to doesn't belong. It was obviously created specifically for the ritual. I can tell because the city does a better job at removing roots and stumps when it plans these places. Not to mention, no city official would think that it was a good idea to make a picnic area over a ley line convergence, even a newborn one like this.

I walk around the clearing again before I crouch, reaching down to touch the charred grass that forms the outer lines of the septagram. The residual magic stings my fingertips, like I've reached into a hornet's nest.

"So? Could a single practitioner have done this?" Aries breaks the silence to ask, though he doesn't move any closer from the tree line. He got this job because of his charisma and his ability to talk the Elyries—particularly, the other Fae—into following the guidelines, not because he has any particular skill or knowledge about rituals.

"No, definitely not," I answer as I finally straighten, eyeing the circle critically. The ground at the center is bone-dry, the little bit of grass remaining charred. A pit sits at the center, cracks spreading outward like lightning. "I'd say you're looking at either twelve low-level casters or seven mid-level. If they were particularly powerful, possibly only three, though I find it unlikely."

Getting even three wixxes to join for a ritual like this—highly illegal, and a power drain if I've ever seen one—should have been nearly impossible. "A coven, most likely, though I haven't heard of any new ones forming lately." Few wixxes were willing to endure the melding of powers necessary to form one. There's the Grand Coven, but they are too bureaucratic to be involved.

"How can you tell?" He finally steps up beside me to stare at the power circle. It's easy to see where the outer ring was intentionally broken, likely by a silver blade. The ground is neatly sliced, the grass withered.

"This is a Faery Star." I don't plan on elaborating. He's Fae, so the meaning should be obvious, but he just stares at me blankly. "Really? Nothing?" He shrugs, so I break it down with a sigh. "It's a septagram...a seven-pointed star. Also called the Seal of Babylon, the Sacred Whore of Thelema. It's an extremely powerful glyph. A novice trying to lay it is more likely to be sucked into the ether than successfully open a portal."

"Portal?" Aries blurts, dark skin blanching. "This was a portal?"

I rub my eyes. *Idiots, the lot of them...even my dear friend.* "Most likely, otherwise it should be a pentagram. They're much more stable. Each point of a pentagram roots the sigil to the earth and the elements. A septagram ties the earth to either Above or Below." I glance at the lines again. "Likely Below, given the fire." I swallow down my dissertation on the Rune and what each point could mean. It's a fascinating topic but not important in the immediate moment.

"What are we looking at then? Demon?" Aries, rightfully so, looks skittish. Any of my kin who are trying to immigrate from Kur need to fill out hundreds of forms, go through evaluation after evaluation and are subjected to dozens of power-dampening spells and restrictions. Illegally entering through a portal is a high crime.

And that's not even mentioning the damage one could do unsupervised. There is a reason that the paperwork rarely gets approved. Only the fact that I'd already been on earth for almost a millennium before the BAA formed had gotten me the exception.

Well, and also, there are few beings, alive *or* dead, who can force me to do anything I don't want to do. The only way they are dragging me back to Kur is as a corpse.

I crouch down again, breathing deeply for a scent. When I catch it, it's faded. "A lesser one. A level nine, maybe a weak eight. If I had to guess, I'd say a pit demon." The weaker ones all smell the same, sulfur and brimstone.

"Shit." Aries swipes his hand through his black hair before glaring at the sky. "Can you tell how long?"

"Since it got out? Several hours at least." Straightening back up, I dust the dirt off my hands before shoving them into my pockets. "Have you checked the police reports?" Pit demons are fairly low in power, but they are still plenty deadly to Blanks. Unless whoever summoned it managed to collar it immediately, there'd be reports of violence skyrocketing somewhere.

"I'll get right on that." Aries snaps his fingers. A young BAA agent runs over from the woods, notebook in hand.

"Yes, Sir Aries?" he asks, out of breath and clearly starstruck.

"I need you to go over all the police reports in a...hundred-mile radius?" Aries glances toward me for approval, and I shrug. A pit demon could have gone farther, but why would they? He turns back to the younger man. "Any spikes in violence, unexplained crimes, anything out of the usual."

"Yes, sir!" The agent snaps off a salute before scurrying away.

Aries turns back to me, rolling his eyes. "Probies."

"You'd have to do your own research without them. And get your own coffee." I know the leanan sidhe has an unhealthy fascination with the bean juice. Ever since he'd sworn off mortal lovers, he'd been drinking too much of the stuff. At least it wouldn't kill him.

"The horror." Aries shudders at the thought. "So, is there anything else you can tell me? Who cast it, anything?"

"Not really. A wix could maybe point you in the right direction. You know I don't dabble." It's only kind of a lie. I don't dabble *anymore*, not since my ex stole my *Focus*. Without it, laying spells takes far too long for me to bother if I don't need to. "If it were me, I'd see who bought powdered moondust or" — I suck in another breath, then sneeze — "a large amount of cinnamon. Trace the ingredients. Can't be too many wixxes buying all of them."

Aries sniffs. "Already got someone on that."

"Then until you track the demon, not much else I can do here." Maybe I'll head into the city for a snack, now that I have a feeder back home and don't need to worry about losing control.

Before I can decide anything, though, the young officer runs back over to Aries. "Sir, there's been a string of bar fights in Old Manhattan!"

"Sounds like a good place to start." Aries grins and claps my shoulder. "Let me know what you find out, and I'll follow up on the circle."

"Don't suppose you've got me a ride?" I ask before leaving.

"Want me to call you a taxi?" Aries jokes.

"Wow, your budget must be huge. I should raise my fee." I waggle my eyebrows at him.

He laughs and tugs out a set of keys, tossing it to me without bothering to look. I snag them out of the air and eye them. "Please be the motorcycle. Please be the motorcycle."

"Oh shut up. You know it is. Now get on with it before I have to fill out even more paperwork." Aries waves me away.

I love Aries' motorcycle. It's a sleek black beast that cost a fortune to import from Europe, and even more to keep topped up with gas, an antique monster from the twenty-first century. They don't make them like this anymore.

I'm not in the city often enough to justify buying and storing one, but I've thought about it.

Gods, have I thought about it.

I swing my leg over the hog and relish the feel of the power between my thighs, rumbling to life as I spin the key in the ignition. "Hello, precious," I murmur, taking a second to enjoy the moment before I finally pull out of the parking spot and onto the street. The only good thing that the Collapse caused was the lack of traffic. Of course, navigating between pedal bikes is nearly as annoying as I remember traffic being, but at least they move slower.

The thrill of speeding down the pavement, wind whipping my hair behind me, reminds me of flying — something else I'm not allowed to do in the city without a hefty fine. The cycle is the closest I can get, so I take full advantage.

It doesn't take long to travel the few miles into Old Manhattan proper. I hardly remember what it used to look like before it became just another slum. The walls are a riot of color, faded graffiti layered under newer, brighter tags, skyscrapers that used to hold offices now crammed full of subsidized housing.

I grin at one such apartment building, not because I enjoy the sight of poverty, but because someone had built a mini version in front of it, complete with ratty awning. It's about five feet wide and almost as high, but I can hear chickens clucking inside. The front is held closed by wires and a lock.

I look away from the chicken coop and realize that I'm about to miss my turn, so I take it sharply, only avoiding overbalancing by luck and a prayer, nearly clipping a container garden on the edge of the sidewalk.

"Watch it, asshole!" a man juggling a sack of groceries hollers as I pass, and I just laugh.

I love Old York.

Chapter Eleven

Pet

I don't know what I did wrong, but when I find out, I'm never doing it again.

Was I too eager? Too unskilled? Should I have tried harder—or had I tried too hard?

Where did I screw up that led me to being dragged back to the basement and shoved into the silver pen again?

I huddle on the bare mattress with my arms wrapped around my knees as I lie in the fetal position, my body seizing. My skin is pink and irritated from scratching it, and my throat feels like I swallowed gravel.

It's been at least three sleeps since they shoved me in here. The first day wasn't bad. Lonely, but no lonelier than the upstairs room—a bit colder, but I feel like I've always been cold. The second day, I woke up with the sore throat. The itching started this morning.

Goddess Moon is singing as she swells, and even down here, I can hear her song. Fear swells in my chest. I won't shift right, I know it—not down here and *definitely* not without Alpha. Already, I can feel my wolf pacing, growling in my belly. Or maybe that's my stomach, since my food sits untouched by the slot in the gate. I can't push down the nausea enough to convince myself to eat.

My skin ripples uncomfortably, and I know it's starting. It feels like spiders crawling underneath my flesh, and I curl my fingers into my palms. I want to scratch my skin off my muscles, rend muscles from bone until the wolf is forced out. My muscles spasm painfully, and I curl into the cramping pain with a cry.

It comes in waves, muscles pulling tight, then releasing, then pulling back tighter as my wolf tries to rip free from my body. I try to breathe through it, to let it out the way Alpha always said to, but I can't...not alone.

I force myself to roll over onto my stomach then shove my body to its knees like it will help, but it just sends a new wave of pain. "Let go," I say through gritted teeth. "Let it out. It won't take over."

My whole body lurches as my femur snaps in my thigh, and I scream at the pain. And then my other one snaps, and I collapse onto my side, my vision going black.

Then I wake up, my body icy but whole, and the whole process starts over again, bones breaking and healing and breaking and healing and no amount of screaming makes it feel better.

Or brings my Alpha to help.

Chapter Twelve

Master

"Three days, Levi," Aries grumbles from across the coffee shop table, his hands curled around a steaming mug. His eyes are shadowed from lack of sleep. It is dark outside the diner windows, the swollen moon gleaming in the cloudless sky. I wonder how my little wolf is faring.

"I've taken out six different demons for you, Aries," I snap back, equally tired. Pit demons aren't particularly hard to kill, but traveling across the city to track them at all hours of the night and day is exhausting. "I don't know what else you expect from me."

"Some help finding the bastards opening the portals would be nice." Aries huffs into his coffee.

Anger swims in my chest at the allusion that I'm somehow to blame. Only our long friendship keeps me from snapping. "I'm not a Summoner. You've got a whole team of bureau lackeys to deal with that. Surely you've found *something*."

"None of the Summoners can tell me how they're doing it. They're willing to admit that whoever laid the first circle was relying on the ley lines, but the last ones were nowhere near an outside power source. They shouldn't have been able to open it so quickly. And they can only find one magical signature, which *you* claim is impossible. We're missing something."

My cellphone starts to vibrate, so I drag it out of my pocket and glance at the screen. "One sec, I gotta take this." I thumb the screen and lift it to my ear.

"The boy's not doing so well," Maggie says in lieu of greeting. "You best be getting back quick."

I sigh and swipe my hair off my face. "I can't come home yet. There's a situation here. He can run outside next month. He'll have to deal for now."

"But—" Maggie sounds aggravated. I know staying inside on the full moon probably doesn't feel great, but there's nothing I can do. Until I find whoever's laying the circles or run completely out of leads, I need to be here. Unfortunately, the latter is looking the most likely.

"I really can't right now, Maggie. Just do what you can." I hang up and shove my phone back in my pocket.

"New pet?" Aries finally grins, probably because he's halfway through his second mug of bean juice.

"A wolf," I reply, grinning as well, thinking back to our time in the garden. Maybe I'll take him for another walk when I get back, an apology for cooping him up through the full moon.

Aries' eyes grow dreamy. "I had one of those once. Beautiful singing voice." I haven't heard Eryn sing. If it sounds anything like the moans he lets out while coming, it would be lovely. "I almost feel bad for calling you away."

"You should. He's delicious."

"Oh, too much information... You know I've gone off sex." Aries pouts and sits back in his chair.

"That's *your* choice." A choice I still didn't understand. A year or two of happiness was surely better than a lifetime alone.

"You might be able to handle watching your lovers die, but I need a break from it." Aries sets his mug roughly down on the table, clearly annoyed, and I suppose I understand. Granted, most of the men who warm my bed leave at the end of the night with coin in their pocket, but I've lost a few over the years by losing control.

As a leanan sidhe, Aries doesn't have that option. Sex is tied to his power. It gives his lover a boost of inspiration, followed by a short life. No opting out, no alternatives.

Prolonged chastity isn't something I could see myself excelling at, but Aries has been handling it well.

"Touché," I concede the point and spin my untouched coffee cup around, enjoying the warmth on my palms. I won't drink it, but Aries always insists I buy one. Something about how sitting empty handed in a coffee shop draws the wrong kind of attention.

I think he just wants a free refill.

A bell dings over the café door, and I glance up at the familiar smell.

Wolf.

Not mine but similar. He's older, rugged with the shadow of a beard. For a moment, I consider sweet-talking him back to my suite at the hotel. There's nothing quite as thrilling as taking a strong alpha wolf and putting him on his knees.

But I can't quite work up the desire. He's attractive, but he's not...mine, which is sure as hell a new feeling for me.

I sigh and slouch back in my chair, twirling my spoon in my bean juice.

Aries chuckles and drains the last of his drink. "Aren't you going to see how well he can bounce on your dick? A big guy like that, and I bet he's all growl, no bite."

"Don't do me dirty, Aries. I'm trying to be good here." I groan and shove my cup across the table to him. Coffee slops over the rim, smearing across the table until he halts the mug with his hand. He takes it with a grateful grin and sips it.

"You've really got it bad, don't you?"

"You would too if you saw his perky little ass."

"Now *you* don't do *me* dirty, Levi." Aries sighs. "Though I bet it is. Okay, you gotta tell me, does it fit in the palm of your—" Before he can finish, his phone vibrates on the table and we both sigh.

"Pit demon?"

He glances at the screen. "Pit demon."

* * * *

The moon is waning before the BAA finally sends in backup, and I can go home. With enough wixxes in Old York City to cover every street corner, they should be able to nip any portals opening in the bud. I can't wait to get home. As pleasant as it is to spend a few days out in the city, I much prefer the comforts of home.

And the solitude, because, good gods, the city is rank.

I crouch down just inside the door of my estate to unlace my leather boots. They are caked with mud and dust. Maybe, if my pet is good, I'll let him clean them. I smile at the thought. My little wolf would look good on his knees in front of me, shining the leather, maybe with a little spit and some elbow grease.

Before I can get too deep into my fantasies, though, Maggie storms out of the next room to loom over me. Her brogue is thick when she finally speaks. "You egotistical, selfish *glaikit*."

"*Glaikit*?" I ask, grinning as I straighten up. She only comes up to my shoulders, but her snarl is fierce and I'm almost scared.

"Idiot!" she snaps, swatting my shoulder. "You go downstairs *right now* and take care of that boy of yours."

I barely restrain myself from rolling my eyes. "Don't worry. I'll take the little wolf for a walk around the yard later. I have to — "

"No, you will go *now*. That poor boy spent the last week miserable and in pain. You will get your ass downstairs and make it better." Maggie plants her hands on her hips and glares in a way that makes it impossible to say no. It's odd to see her so agitated, since she's not typically a person prone to fits of drama.

"Fine, I'll go. Keep your panties on." I squeeze past her and head for the basement stairs. I'm halfway down before I catch the sweet stench of dried blood and realize that Maggie might be right.

Something is wrong.

Chapter Thirteen

Pet

The sound of heavy footsteps comes from the stairs. I force my head to turn, sagging in relief when I see it's Master, finally here. My body aches, every joint screaming at me, and my skin feels like it's on fire, but I don't care. I'll suffer through the pain if it means getting out. As soon as he opens the cage, I scramble off the mattress.

"I'll be good, Sir — *Master*. I will, I really will, I promise." I stumble over my words as I collapse at his feet, dizzy with hunger and pain. I clutch at his knees to keep myself upright before I realize he might not want me to touch him. Maybe that was what put me here in the first place? I release him like a hot coal. "Sorry. Sorry… I didn't mean it. I'm sorry."

"Hey, little wolf, what's the matter? Shh, calm down, everything's fine. Shit, you're covered in bruises. Maggie! *Maggie!*" Master is yelling and I hate it, but I don't know what he wants from me right now. Does he want me to kneel? I don't think so, because a second passes then he grabs my arms just beneath my shoulders, shoving me backward toward the mattress.

Farther from the door.

I start to cry, tears sliding down my cheeks and making my face itch even more than it already does.

"No, don't cry, baby. I'm here. I've got you."

"I...I'll do better." I catch myself clutching at his shirt, but I can't let go. "Please let me go back to the other room. Please don't make me stay in here anymore."

He curses then I feel like I'm flying. His arms are warm around me as he rushes me out of the cage and upstairs before I can cry out. Then, he's laying me on the bed in the blue room. I never thought I'd be happy to see the dreary walls again.

"Maggie!" he hollers once more.

The woman rushes in behind him, tutting over me by the bed. She lays the back of her hand on my forehead. I feel like she's done that before, sometime over the past few days when I was too out of it to notice much — sometime between the third femur break and fourth collarbone. I remember her voice, muttering about idiots and rules meant to be broken.

"I think his fever's finally breaking," Maggie takes her hand off my forehead and strokes it through my hair instead. "Think you can keep something down yet, honey?"

The thought of eating makes me gag, and I shake my head quickly, then whimper as it sends shockwaves of pain through my skull.

"What fever?" Master asks, leaning closer. He smells faintly of smoke and ash, but mostly of leather. "You should have said something —"

"You mean like when I called you and told you that you needed to come home quick to check on him?" Maggie interrupts, and I cower, waiting for him to get angry and yell at her...or worse.

He doesn't. Instead, he almost seems to cringe. I drop my eyes from his face as a vulnerable expression crosses it. "You're right," he admits, and it shocks me enough to glance back up.

He meets my eyes before perching on the edge of the mattress, near me but not touching. "I'm sorry, little wolf. I should have come back. I thought... Well, that doesn't matter." Hesitantly it seems, he cards his fingers through my hair. "Rest. We'll talk later."

I clutch his road-grubby shirt and tug myself closer, ignoring the musty smell as I bury my face against his chest. I'll take a smack or a beating, but I can't deal with him leaving. "Please stay, please. You can bite me again—"

"I'm not going anywhere, Pet. Close your eyes," Master soothes. I don't think I can sleep, no matter how exhausted I feel, but apparently I'm wrong. He keeps petting my hair, and I drift off without realizing it.

* * * *

I don't know how long I sleep, but the room is dark when I wake. I tense up like a bowstring at the thought of being alone, but then I realize that I'm not. Master is sitting on the end of the bed, dangling his legs over the edge, his back against the wall. He has a book open on his knees, but he doesn't seem to be reading it. Instead, he's staring to his left, away from me. There's nothing to look at, though, just a blank wall, which might be why he's frowning.

I shiver, suddenly cold, and the mattress creaks below me.

Immediately, Master is in motion, the book tumbling forgotten to the floor as he pulls the comforter higher on my chest. "I didn't mean to wake you," he says softly. If he was anyone else, I'd say it was guilt on his face.

"You didn't," I rasp, my voice dry.

He reaches down to the floor and picks up a glass of water, holding it to my mouth with one hand while his other cups the back of my head, helping me drink it. It's lukewarm and tastes of chlorine, but I'm so thirsty I gulp it down, coughing as I swallow too quickly.

"Easy, little one," Master gently chides, taking the glass away for a few seconds until the coughing fit eases. "How are you feeling?"

"I'm okay." It's mostly true. Thanks to the water, my throat is less sore, though my voice is still hoarse from the screaming. I glance down, trying to covertly scout out my injuries. I still ache like I've been trampled by a horse, but besides bruises, now a faded sickly green, I seem fine. The hives have disappeared completely.

"No, you're not, are you?" Master sets the glass down, then runs his finger from the bridge of my nose to the tip in a soothing stroke. "I'm sorry, Eryn. I didn't realize you get Moonsick."

The term is new to me, and I frown, picking at the comforter. "I don't know what that is."

"Hmm?" Master looks confused. "You don't shift with the moon, right?" he clarifies, his lips turning down. "I bet you need something to help you — an older wolf to talk you through it or a low dose of wolfsbane?"

"Wolfsbane?" I yelp, shaking my head immediately. "Alpha says — *said*," I correct myself immediately, "never to touch it, that aconite's addicting."

Master scoffs. "It *can* be, if you take it every day. A dose right before the full moon will hardly do anything. It just calms your inner wolf enough to leash it—or so I've heard. But if you've not taken it before, then I'm guessing someone else helped you, right? Like the man who brought you to the market, or..." He lifts his brow, clearly waiting for me to answer.

"Alpha," I whisper, stomach twisting with the reminder of my failure. "He used to help me."

"It's rare, but not unheard of." Master tips my chin up, forcing me to meet his eyes again. "It's nothing to be ashamed of. I just wish I'd known." His face twists with sadness, and he begins to stroke my hair. "You suffered needlessly because of my ignorance. It won't happen again."

I don't know what to say, so at first I say nothing. The silence stretches uncomfortably between us, then tightens like a band around my chest. "I don't know what I did wrong," I finally offer, the words bursting out of me like a startled deer in the forest. "But if you tell me what it was, I won't do it again."

His brow furrows, and I cringe back against the pillow, regretting saying anything. I should have stayed silent.

"You didn't do anything wrong, Eryn. This was all me, I promise," he finally says, his voice soft.

"You put me back in the pen." It's like my mouth has a mind of its own for the moment, speaking without consulting my brain.

"Oh, little wolf, that wasn't a punishment." Master's eyes grow even more gentle. "I got called away. There was a situation in Old York the BAA needed assistance with. I just didn't want you wandering the grounds alone, not until you know my territory better. There are wards in the woods I didn't want you to trip."

"But you were so cold..." I say then trail off, my cheeks heating as I allude to the day in the garden, where he went from man to statue without warning.

Master is quiet, though his fingers continue to stroke through my hair. "It's been...a very long time since I've cared for someone, truly cared." He sighs and looks away. "The garden was...unexpected. I'm ashamed to admit that it spooked me."

"Oh." I shift slightly until my thigh presses against Master's hip. "I guess that makes sense."

Master spares me a smile before he lets loose a breath, pulling his hand away. He stands and brushes his palms on his thighs. Suddenly, I'm cold again. It's too much like he's brushing away my touch.

"Don't worry, little wolf. Now that I know, next month will go easier. I promise. Get some more rest, okay?" He smiles, but it's tight, and I can tell he wants to leave, so I nod. I don't tell him that I don't think I can sleep more or that for the first time in days, I'm starving. I just nod and grip the comforter tighter.

At least I'm not in the basement.

Chapter Fourteen

Master

Maggie is on me before the door is fully latched. "How's the poor boy? Is he feeling better? Should I take him in some soup? I'll take him in some soup."

"He's fine. Let him rest. It's late." It feels like stepping over a land mine as I squeeze past her. She's not happy with the answer. I don't need to see her frown for the message to come across clear. "Maggie, he's fine. He just got Moonsick."

The need to clean off the dust and dirt from my travels has me starting toward my room upstairs but Maggie follows on my heels. "Moonsick? What's that mean? Is it controllable? Does he need a special diet?"

It's sweet that she cares, but all I want to do is take a shower, so I sigh, planting my hand on the bathroom door as I turn to look at her. "Maggie, he'll be fine. Moonsickness isn't common, but it's manageable."

"But what is it?" Maggie presses.

I struggle to dredge up the information, since it's been almost a century since I'd met a wolf with it, and even then it was just in passing. "It's like the wolf is drunk on the moon. It affects everyone a little different. Some people shift too easily but have no control over themselves when they do, but others—like Eryn, if the bruises are any indicator—can't shift without help. The human holds control too tightly so the shift starts but then aborts partway through as the human clenches down. I'll be able to handle it next month. He'll probably be tired and sore for a few days, but there's no lasting damage."

"You're sure? Would a bath help? Should I...?" She keeps talking but I tune her out, considering what she was saying. Getting Eryn into a warm bath, soaping his body free of sweat, soothing him with my hands...

Abruptly, I turn and go back into the blue room. If Eryn is sleeping, I'll leave him be. The door creaks as I push it open. Eryn flinches up on the mattress, clutching at the covers.

"Master? Is everything okay?" His voice is soft and gentle, haunting like a breeze through a willow.

"It's fine. I just wanted to see if you would like to take a bath?"

He perks up, sitting upright with bright eyes. "Really? Can I?" Immediately, his face falls. "There's only a shower."

Which I know, of course. It's a rickety old thing with decent water pressure but little else to recommend it.

"Come on." Holding out my hand, I wait for him to climb out of bed. He's hesitant, like he thinks I'm going to change my mind. Sadness flutters in my belly at yet another sign of how I've failed the little wolf. I don't know why he has struck a chord that none of my other feeders have come close to touching.

When he's finally in front of me, I take his hand, lacing our fingers together, and give a gentle tug to coax him out of the room. He sticks close to my side as we move through the house. I find myself pointing out each room we pass like a tour guide, enjoying the way his eyes widen with each new sight.

I take note of how he slows in front of the solarium and decide to bring him back after the bath, if he's still awake. It's too late in the day to take a trip through the garden, especially in the early winter with wet hair, but it might do him good to be around the greenery inside.

"And this is my room." I open the door and step back to let him through first. His throat shifts with a swallow, but he steps inside, darting his gaze from the Eastlake walnut chest of drawers I bought new back in the early 1800s to the Prudent Mallard Rococo half-tester bed across from it.

"It looks like something out of a holo..." Eryn breathes as he steps inside, reaching his fingers out like he wants to touch before he yanks them back and fists his hand at his side.

"Except for running electricity and updating the plumbing, I haven't bothered to change much lately." I try to see the room from his point of view. Are the heavy brocade curtains adequately period or just ugly? Was the twenty-first century lamp too dim? I fight the urge to tell Maggie to call an interior decorator first thing in the morning. The room was perfectly fine this morning, and I shouldn't care what my feeder, of all people, thinks.

Shouldn't, but I do.

"It's...wow. Everything looks so *real*." Eryn hunches forward to look at the brass handles on the nightstand, and I feel myself flush. He's only inches away from my favorite toys.

Clearing my throat, I try to ignore the image of him opening the door and taking out the lube and dildo to play with. "That's because it is. I bought everything in here new."

"You, um." His skin turns a pretty shade of pink. "How old are you?"

I shrug. "I stopped counting back in my fifteenth or sixteenth century." The pink fades quickly to gray before he looks away. "Come on. Let's get your bath started." I usher him into the attached bathroom, one of the few rooms in the house I *have* modernized. The bathtub is large, with a holo screen built in just above the temperature controls.

I thumb the power switch and set the water temp to just this side of hot, then dig under the sink while the tub starts to fill. "I've got some strawberry bath oil or... Hmm. I don't know what scent this is, but it has bubbles?" I lift both bubbles to show Eryn, who is standing hesitantly by the door.

He just bites his lip. It's so cute that I grin and say, "Never mind. How about we do both?" Dumping a liberal amount of each bottle into the water makes me sneeze at the overwhelming scent of chemicals, but it's worth it to see him smile. "Come here, little wolf. Let's get you in the bath." I'm glad I decide to help him because his leg wobbles as he tries to step into the deep tub, and he nearly falls. Only my hands gripping his tiny waist keep him on his feet, and he sends me a grateful smile.

I'm too busy trying not to moan at the naked flesh under my palms to do more than grunt in reply. I help lower him into the water. The tap automatically shuts off once it's full, and he leans back so the bubbles tickle his chin, letting out an involuntary sigh.

"How's that feel, baby?" I kick myself at the endearment, but it's too late to take it back, and he doesn't seem to notice.

"Feels nice," he says, tipping his head back to soak his hair. All I can see is his face—his eyes are closed peacefully—and his knobby knees like mountains jutting out of the water.

"Don't fall asleep, okay?" I sit down beside the tub. Maybe I should have brought in a book to read but watching him is no hardship.

"'Kay," he agrees, already drifting.

"Hey, none of that, no sleeping." I reach into the water, ignoring how it soaks my sleeves, to urge him to sit up some so he doesn't drown. "Why don't you tell me about yourself, Pet."

He blinks owlishly at me, pouting slightly before his face clears and he blushes. "Like what? I mean, what do you want to know?"

"All I really know about you is that your name is Eryn Laurier and you're nineteen." And that he gets Moonsick, but that's not something I want to remind him of right now, so I keep it to myself.

"There's not really much to tell," He drops his gaze to the water, and I don't need to know him to know he's lying.

"I think there is. I bet you've got lots of interesting stories to tell. What about your family?" I prod, trying to encourage him with a smile. I want to know more about him — and not just to assuage my curiosity of how he ended up where he did.

If anything, the question makes him even more uncomfortable. "I don't have one," he mumbles, not meeting my eyes. "I don't remember much of my mom, except that she…" He trails off, swallowing around the words before he tries again. "I don't think she liked that I was a… That I'm a wolf. She said we were going to go swimming, but she pushed me under and kept holding me down and calling me a monster and…" He chokes on a sob and turns his back to me. "I don't want to talk about this anymore."

"Oh baby, I'm sorry. You don't have to talk about it." I reach out and stroke over his back in soothing circles, guilt at bringing up a bad memory warring with anger that a mother would try to murder her own child for something so completely out of their control. It makes me want to hunt her down and show her what a *real* monster looks like.

"What's your favorite color?" I finally blurt, anything to make him think about something else.

He's quiet for a bit before he finally turns back toward me and says, "Green. It makes me think of growing things."

"You like gardening?" Grabbing one of the washcloths of the little shelf, I squirt a dollop of soap on it and start to wash Eryn's left arm, moving it in circles from his shoulder to elbow, slowing over each scratch and bruise, then to his wrist. I work it slowly, methodically, down his hand, over his palm, between each finger. I reach for his other arm, and he passes it to me, watching the motion of my hands.

"I don't know. I think so. I didn't get to try at the pack. I was always in someone's way, but I liked to watch the wildflowers grow in the woods." He flips his hand over for me to wash his palm, his face falling. "Especially the lilies..."

"Tell me about the wildflowers," I prompt as I continue washing him. I'm not in a hurry. I'm finding a surprising amount of joy in cleaning him up. It's almost as much fun as getting him dirty, but I pull my thoughts from that before they can go too much further, since keeping everything clean is hard enough when he's naked beneath my hands.

"There are these really pretty purple ones that grow by the hill in the valley, called echinacea. The goldfinches love them. They have these long, drooping petals. And um...another purple one is the New England aster. It's even brighter. I don't like it as much because it's too bold, but it's still pretty. My favorite is the—" His words cut off in a gasp as I run the washcloth over his dick. It plumps in my hand, and I stroke him slowly.

"Go on. Tell me your favorite flower, pretty boy," I urge him, abandoning the washcloth to take him in hand, soaping him up gently, my fingers a loose, curling tease.

So much for keeping things clean.

"Um... It's...the bachelor's button. Some people call it a cornflower." He juts his hips upward, thrusting into my hand with a broken moan, then finally meets my eyes with a pleading gaze.

"I know that one," I say, smiling lazily as I keep my strokes slow and teasing, like watching him fall apart isn't pushing me closer to spilling as well. "Did you know that young men in love used to wear it through a buttonhole? If it wilted too quickly, then it was a sign their love was unrequited. That's how it got its nickname."

"I— No, I didn't know that." Eryn jerks as I twist my hand around the head of his dick, a keening cry slipping through his lips. "Please, Master," he cries out, hands gripping the sides of the tub.

"You know what I like about cornflowers?" I say, not acknowledging his plea. As I ask, I flick my thumb over his weeping slit, smoothing the silky pre-cum over his fiery hot skin. Even under the water, I can feel him leaking, which makes me even hotter. "They're such a pretty blue, just like your eyes."

He closes them immediately, his face flushed in either embarrassment or arousal.

"No, baby. Open them back up for me. Let me see you." I slide my other hand over his hip and up his chest, flicking his budded nipple with my thumb. He arches his back immediately. "So sensitive," I murmur.

He obediently opens his eyes, meeting mine with difficulty.

"Such a good boy." The praise feels good on my tongue and makes him go boneless. With a cry, he spills in my hand, his hips stuttering as he pumps his pearly fluid into the water. "There you go, baby. Doesn't that feel nice? Such a good boy for me."

I help him stand on shaky legs, stepping right into the tub with him, despite my clothing. If I'd been thinking, I'd have washed his hair before I brought him to climax, but he looked so sweet and innocent talking about wildflowers that I couldn't resist dirtying him up. I flick the drain open with my toe, then fiddle with the shower controls.

The warm water starts to rain down on us, and I coax him to lean against me as I work the shampoo into a lather in his hair, helping him rinse it, then repeat the process with conditioner.

He's so blissed out, riding the aftershocks of his orgasm, that I practically carry him. Supporting his weight with one arm, I dry him off then guide him onto my bed while I strip myself of my soaked clothing and change into a pair of silk night pants. He's sleeping when I finish, curled around my pillow.

I know I should wake him, take him back to the blue room, but I can't. Not for the first time since he's arrived, I see him as more than a feeder. It's why I try to keep my distance from them, why they stay in their space and I in mine, but it's too late.

So rather than wake him, I carefully tug the blankets from beneath him and tuck him in, brushing a strand of hair off his face.

I'm so fucked.

Chapter Fifteen

Pet

Pain, sharp but fleeting, wakes me. A steel bar around my waist keeps me from flinching away but it doesn't stop my heart from pounding with fear. Then, before I can do more than tense, it's over. Master lifts his mouth from my neck and murmurs, "Good morning, baby."

"Master?" It's both a question and a plea, and I don't know what I'm asking for, but I know if he doesn't answer, I might break.

"Did you sleep well?" he asks, and it's not the answer I want but it's not the one I feared, either.

"Did...did you bite me?" My voice is small.

"Just a little nip." He purrs, sliding his tongue over my skin. It sends a shiver down my spine, and my cock hardens against my thigh. "You don't mind, do you?"

I don't know how I feel. If he'd woken me up with his cock in my mouth—or mine in his—I'd have no complaints, but this seems different...bigger, more dangerous. The feel of his fangs in my skin is both erotic and terrifying, a cycle that leaves me more confused than anything.

He sighs when I don't answer, his breath skimming my skin. "Would you rather I wait until you wake?"

"Yes, please," I whisper, burying my face in the pillow as I hope the answer won't send me back to the cage in the basement.

"Okay, little wolf," he agrees, dropping a kiss to the nape of my neck. "Time to get up now so you can get *your* breakfast." The thought of food has me sitting up so abruptly that I get dizzy, and he chuckles. "Not so fast, baby. I promise there's no rush."

My stomach disagrees. It growls, loud and angry, and I press my hand against it to quiet it. Master climbs gracefully off the bed, then holds out his hand until I tentatively take it. He pulls me along with him, and we end up downstairs in a formal dining room, at a table for twelve set for two. We barely sit down before a girl hustles out, a steaming plate in one hand. She's wearing a black dress with white tights and a matching frilly white apron.

She is silent as she puts the plate down in front of me, politely ignoring the napkin I have draped over my lap. She gives Master a nervous curtsy until he waves her away.

"You're not eating?" I ask, unwilling to grab my fork until he's given me permission. It looks delicious, and I can barely hold back from scooping the diced potatoes and leaking eggs into my mouth.

The look he gives me is amused. "I already ate, remember?"

My skin heats at the reminder, but I clarify. "I mean, I know that, but don't you eat real food too sometimes? For appearances?" The vampires that came to the packhouse didn't eat *much*, but they'd always sampled the food as a courtesy, at least.

Maybe he just doesn't want to put on a front in his home?

His nose scrunches up in obvious disgust. "I have no need to fill my mouth with decaying carcasses. You, however, should eat before it gets cold. I've heard it tastes better that way."

Permission granted, I start shoveling food into my mouth, barely pausing to swallow. I'm starving, even when my fork drags along my empty plate. Only then do I realize with embarrassment the way he is watching me. I drop the fork and look down.

"Are you still hungry?" he asks, not seeming to care that I'd just done an impression of a food vacuum.

I nod then shrug, not quite willing to lie.

"Wait here, sweetheart. I'll get you more." Master takes my empty plate and carries it out of the room, leaving me alone at the table. The dining room seems colder immediately, the walls shifting outward to loom around me. Hunching farther into my chair doesn't make the room any less oppressive but makes me feel better.

Master is back with a new plate of food before long, setting it in front of me. "Go ahead and eat up."

Slowly at first, I obey, picking at my food, the opposite of my earlier display, but the taste quickly overwhelms my uncertainty. This time, I can't clear my plate. I poke at the last, lonely strip of bacon. I hate the idea of wasting food, but my stomach claims it will burst if I take even one more bite.

"You're looking at that like it personally offended you." Master laughs and takes the plate before I can force myself to eat it. "I'll dispose of it for you."

"I just don't want to waste it." The words come out leaking apology from every syllable.

"The Nightmares will eat it. It won't get wasted. Trust me." Master winks and disappears again.

I wait impatiently at the table for him to return, no longer worried about the opulence now that I know he has Nightmares. Will he let me see them? Can I pet one or, even better, maybe *ride* one?

I feel like I'm bouncing by the time he returns. "Can I see the Nightmares?" I ask before he makes it more than partway into the room. "I'll be good, I promise. I just want to see one and maybe pet it, if you let me. Are they as big as I've read they are? The books say some are friendly. Will they let me ride them?"

Master is clearly taken aback by the deluge of words, but after a second, he grins. "Mine are fairly tame. I suppose it wouldn't hurt anything to introduce you."

* * * *

The Nightmare is surprisingly tiny. "He's...smaller than I expected," is the first thing I say, from my position just behind Master. He's so much bigger than me that I have to crane my body at the waist to peer around him.

"He's still a colt." Master crouches down into the straw and holds his hand, palm down, toward the hip-high foal—my hip, not his. The black horse tucks his muzzle beneath the palm for scratches, huffing out a happy-sounding sigh. His mane, a twisting stream of shadows and smoke, billows over his neck.

We're out in the stables, tucked beside a large fenced-in meadow. It smells of ash and dust and manure, but it's cleaner than I expect. Clean or not, I'm grateful for the dark gray sweatpants and oversized shirt master lent me to wear in the stables, and *more* grateful for the shoes, even if they are a size too big.

"He's beautiful." And he is, though his sharp teeth make me squirm. "Does he bite?"

"He hasn't yet. I don't expect him to, to be honest. I bred him from a soft line."

With that reassurance, I drop to my knees and run my fingers along the fur on the colt's neck. It's soft as velvet but warm. "Hi, baby," I coo at him, and nickers in reply, butting into my hand.

Master places his hand over mine and guides it down to the Nightmare's shoulder. "Scratch here."

I obediently curl my fingers into the fur and the colt's whole body shudders, weight leaning heavily into my hand. "Oh, you love that." I purr at him, repeating the movement again, until he gets so excited that a giant glob of drool drips from his lips onto my bare shoulder.

It's disgusting, but I laugh anyway. Master stands to grab a hand towel hanging on a hook on the wall, then crouches to clean the stickiness off me. "Now that he's christened you, I think it's safe to say he likes you."

That makes me smile even more as I go back to petting the beautiful creature. "Do you ride them?"

"Sometimes. Not as much lately… I've been caught up in the house. I should come out more." Master reaches out and pats the colt's neck. "His sire is my usual mount, actually."

"Did you hear that, baby? Your daddy is his favorite." I coo again at the colt. "What's his name?"

"He doesn't have one. I was intending to sell him but haven't found the right buyer. Too many beings want them for the wrong reasons." Master drags his fingers along the little creatures neck, smoothing out the fur. "He wouldn't survive a Blood Sport."

I shudder at the thought of the gentle beast in pain and shift closer, cooing words of reassurance that I have no way of backing up. I could stay out here for hours, but unfortunately, Master twists his wrist to look at his watch, and I know my time is running short. I give the horse a final rub before I stand back up. "Is it time to go back inside?"

Master reaches out to scratch the colt. "Not yet. Come on. Let's go meet his daddy."

Something about him saying that word sends a quiver through me. Was it because I was remembering how he called himself that as he stroked his thick cock in front of my face? Or something else?

If he notices, he doesn't comment. He leads me farther into the stable to a stall about halfway down. The doors here are reinforced steel, but I can see the divots and dimples, like the creature behind them was strong enough to nearly punch through. Each mark is as large as a dinner plate.

"Stay here," Master orders, stopping me a few feet off to the side. "I'll bring him out." He opens the door just wide enough to slip inside and instantly, the air is filled with what sounds like screaming as the Nightmare greets him. It quiets quickly, and I hear Master murmuring, then what sounds like leather dragging over the cement ground.

Finally, the stall door opens farther and Master steps out, his tall frame dwarfed by the horse-like creature attached to the lead in his hand. I've read about Nightmares, but the diagrams in the books did nothing to prepare me for how large a full-grown one really is. Master's head barely grazes the beast's shoulder. Mine would be lucky to come partway up his side. His saddle is black leather with red stitching that matches the fiery eyes. Unlike the baby, who danced playfully and shook his smoke-and-shadow mane, this Nightmare stands tall and proud.

"Beautiful," I breathe out, rocking forward on my toes, barely restraining myself from running forward. "What's his name?"

"Damsel," Master answers immediately and I snort, thinking it's a joke, but Master only grins. "It used to be Apollo, but he spent so much energy trying to get into Distress' stable that I changed it." I must look confused because he chuckles. "Get it? Damsel *in* Distress?"

My laugh barks out of me, and I slap my hand over my mouth to smother it. It's such a dumb joke, one I never thought someone like him would make.

"You can laugh." Master crosses his arms, the lead still gripped tightly in his hand, and I can't help it. The thought of a magnificent beast like the Nightmare being named Damsel is just too silly. When I finally stop, Master lifts a brow. "Would you like to ride him?"

"By myself?" I yelp, my laughter dying. I don't think my legs will even stretch far enough to sit comfortably in the saddle. There's no way I'll be able to stay up there.

"If you want...or with me."

"With you, please," I reply, and Master nods. He waves me over, and I approach carefully, my eyes fixed on the Nightmare's sharp teeth. Damsel is ignoring me, though, staring imperiously toward the barn door. Master slides his heavy leather boot into the stirrup and swings his right leg over the horses back until he can settle into the saddle gracefully. Then, he stretches his left hand toward me.

I grab it.

Somehow, he manages to effortlessly lift me onto the saddle in front of him. My feet dangle. Even if I wanted to, they wouldn't reach the stirrups, and I can already feel the burn of the stretch in my thighs. I ignore it in favor of the heat coming up through the saddle and the warmth of Master at my back.

He keeps hold of the reins in his left hand but presses his right to my stomach, urging me farther back until I'm plastered against him. "Just move with me, baby. I won't let you fall."

I feel him shift behind me, then Damsel is strolling slowly out of the barn. Once we're in the meadow, he clicks his tongue, and the Nightmare shifts into a trot. His gait is surprisingly smooth for such a big creature, and Master's arm around my waist is as secure as a safety belt.

"We can stay in the yard, or if you'd like, we can go out back to the trails." Master offers me the choice.

"Trails, please," I answer quickly, excited about getting to see the woods.

He pulls gently on the reins and turns us toward the trees. As we head through the tall grass — not that it looks tall compared to the Nightmare's lanky form — Master's breath tickles my ear. "There's a bed of wildflowers near the pond. I'm sure you're not interested, but…" His amusement is clear.

"I am! I am! Can we see them? What kind?" I'm bouncing in the saddle, until Damsel huffs and I force myself to still.

"There's some black-eyed susans and some dwarf-lake irises. There's a little patch of witch's bell, I believe. You'll have to tell me the names of some." Master's voice is a deep purr.

"Yes," I agree, my own voice breathy.

"It's a pity it's too cold to swim," Master muses once we reach the tree line, stepping into the shadows. Now that he mentions it, it is a bit chilly, but the Nightmare is putting off enough heat to combat most of the discomfort. I find myself grateful for the excuse to stay out of the water. Will he think less of me when he knows of the terror that swarms me at the thought of swimming? Of how easily someone could drag me under and steal away my breath?

"That's *tradescantia ohiensis*." I gesture to the three-petaled purple flower growing just to the side of the path, forcing my mind from the unnecessary fear. "Also called spiderwort."

"Pretty," Master murmurs into the nape of my neck, and I wonder if he even looked. I continue to point out different species of wildflowers as we meander down the trails. They get narrower the deeper into the woods we go, though not so narrow as to give Damsel problems.

Master slows a few times to show me things, as well. "See that gold shimmer in the air?" I follow his finger to see what he means. It almost looks like a swarm of fireflies, but not as bright. More like glitter. "That's one of the wards. If it's gold like that, it won't hurt you. If you cross it, it'll just be a minor enthrallment. You'll find yourself staring at a mushroom for hours until someone stumbles on you."

A bit later, he points at a shadow cast in the wrong direction. "If you trip one of those, it'll send you floundering in the opposite direction of where you are heading until you find yourself wandering around in circles."

He continues to show me the wards and eventually, I ask, "Why are there so many?" I don't ask why he is showing me, since I don't want him to change his mind. But surely, he wouldn't want me to know they were here? Isn't he worried I'll run? I mean, I won't, but I *could*. Unless there are more traps, worse ones, that he hasn't shown me.

"I used to have a lot of enemies, and these would keep trespassers occupied until I could deal with them. Most of them have died or moved away, but I find it better to be safe than sorry." He says it so matter of factly that I find myself relaxing, even if the talk of enemies is kind of scary. What kind of person has *enemies?*

A rich one, I realize, the answer obvious.

Chapter Sixteen

Master

I swing out of the saddle before helping Eryn down, hands under his arms until he's steady on his feet, which takes a second. Then I use a manger knot to tie Damsel's reins to a sturdy tree branch, near enough to a patch of grass to graze but not too near the thickets. He loves to eat the thorny bushes, but they give him terrible gas. I'd rather not smell it the whole ride back.

Then, I turn to Eryn. He's standing where I left him, shifting his weight from one foot to the other. The sweats he's wearing are too long, landing in folds over the tennis shoes. It's cute. It's even cuter the way he's fiddling with the hem of his shirt.

I make a mental note to buy him some clothes that actually fit.

"Come with me." I hold out my hand, waiting for him to take it before I lead him down another trail, this one far too narrow for Damsel to have fit without knocking his head into branches and trampling the underbrush.

The wildflower bed isn't far. It's small, tucked in a small pool of sunlight that manages to slip through the canopy overhead. It's a pretty riot of colors that gives off a gentle fragrance. Eryn's whole face lights up as he drops to his knees beside it, careful to avoid crushing any of the delicate blossoms.

"This one here is... And this one... I've never seen it in person. I thought it only grew near the old Great Lakes." His mouth gets a little moue as he stares at the tall plant with its fluffy pink flowers. "It looks like astilbe, but...it can't be. They died out in the late sixties. I swear they did."

He looks so confused that I take pity on him and crouch beside him. "I've owned this property since the nineteenth century, under one name or another. A lot of the industrialization that happened through the rest of the state missed here. You could be right." I reach out and brush the soft pink petals. "I don't know their names."

The tip of his tongue peeks between his plush pink lips for a second before he speaks. "Are we in one of the Provinces?"

After the Collapse, the federal government disbanded for several years. Each of the states became, essentially, tiny nations. When the Canadian government got footage of a real, genuine Ice Dragon coming out of hibernation after a thousand-year sleep, the Elyries tried to hush it up. We underestimated the speed with which the footage would make its way through social media. I still remember the mayhem as, one after another, us Elyries were forced out of hiding. Of course, the Blanks called us Supernaturals — too much daytime television, not enough communication to figure out what we called ourselves. It was pure chaos.

It took nearly a decade to put together some semblance of order. Europe, of course, got there first. They formed their own special branch of the EU called S.T.A.R.S. The Supernatural Tracking and Registration Squad. It started out exactly as it sounds — tracing Supernaturals and forcing them to register, monitoring the movements of those deemed 'safe' enough to live in society and removing the rest. It has changed since then, more paperwork and less violence, but the name has stuck.

It took the American States another five years to even agree on a new governing system — a coalition of equal states with their own laws and tax systems who come together only to represent the American States in foreign diplomacy.

Some states, like Texas, kept their name and flag and most of their legislature with minimal changes. Others didn't. It'd been a Kur of a time dealing with the changes, as the entire Great Lakes Region fell apart. By the end of the twenty-first century, the state of Michigan had separated into two Provinces, half of Illinois declared itself independent and Wisconsin, calling itself Greenbay, tried to lay claim to Lake Michigan. It didn't stick — the claim or the name — but it was fun while it lasted.

"We're in Brekkan," I finally answer. "In the thumb."

"So we must be pretty close to the lake then? Is it as big as it looks on maps?" Eryn finally looks away from the wildflowers to look at me with undisguised curiosity, and perhaps a tinge of fear.

"Maybe we can visit in the spring," I reply. "The water is too cold to swim until summer, but I think you'll still like it."

"I'd like that." His smile is wobbly, but his eyes are brighter than the sun above us. I can't help but smile back.

"Tell me more about these flowers," I finally say, breaking eye contact to stop the blush that wants to stain my cheeks. I haven't blushed since…ever. I'm not going to start now.

* * * *

We've missed lunch and nearly dinner by the time I return Damsel to the stables and lead Eryn inside. "Go shower off the horse sweat," I say, gently pushing him toward his room. "Leave the clothes on the floor by your door, and Maggie will have them cleaned. When you're finished, come on out again. I'll scrounge up some food."

His smile is bright. Clearly, he likes the idea of eating with me instead of in his room. Maybe I should break my rules a little longer. I've already let myself get closer to him than I usually do.

Maggie's in the kitchen when we go in. Eryn says a quiet, "Hello," but doesn't stop, obediently going into his room.

"You were out for a while," Maggie comments once the door is closed, her voice bland.

"I showed him the trails. Wanted him to see the wards," I say, as if that were the only reason to spend hours out together.

"Mm," she hums noncommittally.

Tugging open the fridge door, I stare at the shelves stocked full of ingredients I don't know what to do with. "I don't suppose there's anything in here you just throw in the oven…" I muse.

"Hopeless boy, why are you even in my kitchen?" Maggie tuts and elbows me out of the way, grabbing a container of something pink and fleshy and a bag of greens. "I'll feed your pet. You set the table."

"Yes, ma'am," I agree immediately. This way I don't have to worry about accidentally poisoning him.

It takes me three tries to find the right cabinet, but I eventually do. I grab down a plate before hunting for the silverware. "Napkins, too," Maggie prods when I'm about to head to the dining room, so I grab one from the counter. "Clean ones," she scolds, so I sigh, dropping it and digging through yet another drawer. I lift one out for inspection and she nods, waving me away.

By the time I set the table, Eryn is standing in the doorway. I urge him over to his chair and pull it out for him to sit. "Let me go grab dinner. You stay here. Do you want something to drink? Milk, juice, water?"

"Can I have juice?" he asks politely, so I bring out the bowl of what Maggie called 'salad' and a glass of apple juice. Filling his plate with the greens gives me something to do with my hands, which is why I prolong it more than I should.

Eventually, though, I have to take my seat. He takes a bite and a little moan leaks from his lips, making me harden instantly. Subtly, I reach below the table to adjust myself in my jeans, hoping he won't notice. He stays concentrated on his salad.

And I stay concentrated on him, at least until my small furry devil cat leaps onto the table, knocking over

Eryn's glass of juice. It spills over the table and into my lap. I curse, jerking to my feet and swiping at it with a napkin.

"Damn cat. I should have Maggie put you in a stew," I threaten the furry beast.

Lucifer just slowly blinks at me before sitting, his tail flicking, in front of Eryn's plate. Eryn stares at the cat with wide eyes. I know he's not afraid. He's a wolf. It would be irrational.

"You have a cat?" he finally asks, breaking eye contact with the creature to stare at me.

I sniff. "More like, she has me. She showed up on the doorstep last year and just...won't...leave."

Lucifer gives a pitiful meow. The orange and white tabby has me wrapped around her little paw. With a sigh, I use the salad tongs to pull out a piece of meat and drop it onto the tablecloth at her feet. She sniffs at it imperiously before deigning to eat it.

"You like her." Eryn grins as he says it, reading me like an open book. "I bet you named her and everything."

"Lucifer...damn devil cat." I sniff again and pointedly look away from his smirk. It doesn't stop me from hearing the chuckle he chokes back. I sigh. "Go ahead. Laugh. She only looks innocent, I swear. Wait until it's three in the morning and you have to pee." I pretend to shudder. She's tangled up my ankles more times than I can count. I swear she's trying to quietly murder me.

It's as if she knows she's a beneficiary if I die.

"You're a good girl, aren't you?" he coos at her, and when I look, I see him scratching below her chin. She lifts it to give him better access, purring audibly at the

attention. Then, she side-eyes me, as if to say, "*Look...
He sees that I am a Goddess among men.*"

"Don't trust her," I start to say, "She—" Before I can
finish, she clamps her little teeth into his hand, hisses
and dives off the table. "Bites."

"Gets it from her daddy," Eryn says, staring fondly
after the cat while massaging his hand.

"Let me see. If she broke the skin, we'll need to put
some cream on it." I take his hand and examine it. It's
red but not bleeding, so no bandage necessary. Still, I
impulsively kiss the mark. "All better."

He flushes, staring at his hand when I release it.
"Finish eating, baby," I encourage. "I'll clean this up
while you do." Pushing away from the table, I flee to
the kitchen for a washcloth to sop up the spilled juice
and give myself a second to calm down.

Gods, he'd be such a *good* boy.

Chapter Seventeen

Pet

We had such a fun day that I'm disappointed when, after dinner, all Master does is walk me to the blue room and leave me with nothing but a "Goodnight, Eryn." He doesn't even wait to hear my whispered reply. It was weird to hear my name on his lips. I asked him before not to call me 'Pet', but now, I miss it.

I flop back onto the mattress and stare at the ceiling. I hate this room.

I list everything I hate about it, from the bland blue walls to the boring white ceiling to the clinical carpeting until I fall asleep, then list them again in the morning when I wake up and wait for my breakfast. At least my bruises are finally gone, though now my thighs ache from the time spent in the saddle.

Worth it, though.

The next day, the ache is worse, and I wonder how much of it stems from my loneliness. And, I admit, a low-grade fear that I've been abandoned again. The day after, the pain's not so bad. After a week, I don't feel it anymore, but I wish I did, if it means not being so isolated. Even Maggie doesn't stay long, and when she does visit, her eyes are filled with pity.

I thought we had a good day, wandering the woods, but maybe I bored him. Maybe he regrets letting me meet his Nightmares and babble about wildflowers. I shouldn't be surprised. Master spent an entire day with me. It was more time than anyone in my pack ever spent with me by choice, except Alpha, and Alpha was always busy with running the pack. I shouldn't have expected Master to be able to deal with me, either. I need to be grateful that he lets me sleep in a bed and eat such good food instead of table scraps.

My sigh is loud. I feel restless and antsy, filled with too much energy but nothing to expend it on. My foot taps on the mattress, knee bouncing, but nothing helps. I've never spent so long inside in my life.

I start listing the scientific names of all the wildflowers I saw last week alphabetically. I'm on *rudbeckia* when the door cracks open. I look up quickly as Master slips inside. He smiles when he sees I'm awake, like no time has passed. "Come on. I want to show you something."

Anything is better than lingering in this room, so I roll off the bed and follow him. He leads me to a nice living room on the other side of the house. The furniture is just as old as his bedroom set and just as fancy as the dining room, but a small mountain of cheap cloth shopping bags sprawl across the wood coffee table.

"I guessed your size, so if something doesn't fit, just start a pile." Master grabs the first bag and practically shoves it at me. It takes me a second to realize he's not angry. He's embarrassed.

It allows me to take the bag with a small smile and peer inside, when all I want to do is freeze up and wonder what's inside.

It's clothing.

There were shorts I won't be able to wear until spring, sweaters with bright print, jeans in nearly every color, even briefs and brightly colored jocks. The pile of things that fit is significantly larger than the things that don't by the time I get to the last thing he hands me. It's a hanger connected to a heavy bag, and when I unzip the front, I see a suit.

"This," he says before I can even take it out, "will need tailoring. My man will be here soon. I had to go into the city to find the right one." Which explained his absence, even if I wish he'd told me he was leaving. I suppose he doesn't owe me an explanation, just because I want one.

"A suit?" I ask, clutching it but not daring to take it out.

"I'd like to take you somewhere this evening, somewhere nice. You'll need it." He clears his throat and won't meet my eyes.

"I've never worn one before," I admit. I've never owned one, never *dreamed* of a situation where I would need one.

"I'll help you," he immediately offers, stepping forward to help peel the suit out of the bag, setting aside each piece. "Just…let me dress you?"

I nod, biting my lip as he carefully helps me dress, piece by piece. I don't even recognize myself when I look down. I think it fits perfectly but Master frowns critically. "Can take it in at the waist, I think." Then, he kneels in front of me and runs a finger from my knee up my inner thigh, stopping just centimeters from the tent I've created in the groin. "Shorten the inseam a bit," he says, but smirks at me, and I know he's no longer thinking of the tailoring. "You look good in a suit, little wolf." His eyes fill with fire as his smirk turns cocky. "And yet you'd still look better out of it."

His hand is on my thigh, and his mouth? *Gods…it's so close.*

I can't help it. My hips roll toward him, and he chuckles. "That looks uncomfortable, baby. Want some help?"

"Please, Master," I beg, and he doesn't make me wait. He lowers my zipper and fishes out my cock. It looks small in his large hand, and I flush. From the hungry look on his face, I don't think it bothers him.

Then he leans forward and swallows me down to the root, and I no longer care how big I'm not. His mouth is so warm, the suction intense, and when he cups my balls in his hand, that's it. Less than ten seconds and I'm spilling without warning down his throat.

"I'm sorry. Sorry…" I mumble on repeat, embarrassment flooding me, even as the pleasure soars. I should have warned him…or lasted longer.

He gives me a final suck, flicking his tongue over my slit, then he lets me slip from his mouth. "Nothing to be sorry for, little wolf. You are absolutely delectable."

The praise makes me flush even harder, my face burning. He tucks me back into my new briefs and zips me up. I'm barely decent before a servant, a man I haven't met yet, peeks into the room, his cheeks pink. "The tailor's here, Master Levi."

"Send him in," Master says as he stands, meeting my eyes just as he licks a drop of white from his lips and winks. If my face gets any hotter, it will definitely catch fire.

The tailor is an elderly man with a crooked back but straight fingers, and he has the suit pinned for alterations before I can get uncomfortable. The only awkwardness is stripping in front of him to hand it over so he can get started. He leaves in a hurry, muttering about timetables and rush jobs.

As soon as he's out of the door, the tension between me and Master skyrockets. It's heady, warming the air between us until I feel sweat slipping down my bare chest. Master follows the bead with his gaze.

My own trails down his body, over the tight shirt and even tighter black jeans, his arousal straining, impossible to miss. I step toward him, my mouth parting as I stare. "Can I suck you?"

Not just to return the favor, though I definitely want him to feel as good as I did. But I've been dreaming of it, of feeling his thickness on my tongue, tasting his salty release again. Not even his week-long absence could curb it.

Master leans against the side of the couch, gripping the armrest. "On your knees. Right here." He reaches behind him to grab a pillow, dropping it onto the floor at his feet and in seconds, I'm kneeling atop it, my eyes fixed on the straining zipper. "Take me out. Slowly," he orders.

I lower the zipper carefully, and it opens *achingly* slow, and he's still too big to work through the gap, so I pop the button of his jeans as well. His length springs out. He's a big man, so I know he's probably proportional, but his size is still intimidating.

I want to do a good job...the *best* job. I want him to feel as good as he made me feel. I want it to be perfect, but I know I'll have to settle for competent, so I lean forward, prepared to take him, but his hand fists in my hair instead, halting me.

"Not yet. I didn't say you could taste me yet."

Why is it so hot, the way he stops me? He moves my head where he wants it to the crook of his hip, nose buried behind his balls. "Breathe me in, baby. I want you to know how I smell, how I *feel*, before you taste me."

The whimper bursts out of me without warning, out of my control. It's so fucking hot the way he speaks to me, like I am somehow both the center of his universe at this exact moment but also something he *owns*.

I want him to own me.

The collar at my throat seems to tighten in reminder that he does, and it doesn't scare me anymore.

"What do I smell like?" Master asks, his voice stern, demanding an answer, so I breathe in, senses flaring, opening to his scent.

"Sweaty, but…clean. I can smell your bodywash… sage and cedar," I answer. There's more than that, but I can't describe it. I settle for, "Good, Master. You smell *good*."

"Mm. And how do I feel?"

"Hard," I answer immediately, not needing to think. His skin is like velvet, cool and smooth, especially here. I turn my face the smallest degree, as much as he'll let me, to rub my cheek against his hard shaft, and I don't think I imagine his moan. "Warm."

He releases my hair. "Go ahead and find out how I taste, baby."

"Yes, Master." His permission all I needed, I dive on his cock, no longer caring about my inexperience or my nerves. He tastes salty and bitter but not bad, *never* bad.

He fills my mouth just a bit too full and the weight on my tongue is everything I imagined and more.

When the head of his dick bumps the back of my throat, I can't fight down the gag. I think he'll be mad, but then he moans and holds me in place, and I realize he likes it, the feel of my throat convulsing around him.

I might have just come, but my body is singing for him. I want him in me as far as he'll go, leaving his seed in my belly like a scent marker.

He grips my throat, curling the other hand in my hair as he guides my lips almost off his shaft before thrusting in again, using my mouth. I realize I don't *need* to be experienced, that I can be what he wants just by being *here*, like this, on my knees at his feet. He takes my mouth and claims it.

"So good, baby," he pants, his hips always moving, fingers tight in my hair, but the spark of pain only brings me higher, my dick throbbing as hard as ever, and something in my face must make him realize how much I like it because he tugs the strands with a deliberateness that had been lacking previously. His eyes burn into mine, and I find myself caught, unable to look away.

My moan is loud and wrecked, even smothered as it is by his cock, and either the sound or the vibration tips him over, flooding my mouth with his spend. He pumps his load into my mouth, coating the back of my tongue and throat, and I hurriedly swallow, trying not to waste a single drop.

His cock is still hard when he pulls it from my lips, then he's shoving me onto my back, forcing his weight between my thighs, though I give no protest. He loosens his hand from around my throat to slide down my chest and hips, bypassing my throbbing cock to dip lower. I tense as his finger swirls around my hole, a place I've only touched briefly before chickening out.

"Can I make you come on my finger?" Master asks, circling relentlessly but not pushing in, not yet. *Not without my permission*, a thought that makes something terribly like affection well in my chest. He didn't have to ask, I realize. The contract I signed without reading had been explained in explicit detail by the jinni after. That signature is all the permission he needs to do whatever he wants.

But he still asked.

The more he circles, the better it feels, my fear diminishing until finally, I nod. "Yes, Master."

He swipes the finger over the head of my leaking dick, soaking it in pre-cum before he returns it to my entrance, leaning down to take my dick in his mouth for the second time today, just as he presses inside.

I tense but he doesn't stop, moving in relentlessly. It burns, but not as bad as I expect. The pain is just enough to keep me from blowing immediately, enough to keep me hard until the burn subsides to a mere sting then blossoms into a strange pleasure.

And he brushes over some magical place inside me that sends lightning to every nerve ending in my body and again, I spill without warning into his mouth with a scream.

My hips jerk up, fingers clenching into the carpet beneath me, the only thing that keeps me from grabbing him and holding his mouth on me. It *doesn't* stop me from spasming, clenching around his finger even tighter until the aftershocks fade, and I go boneless.

His finger is still inside me when a throat clears from the doorway, and I freeze.

"Sir? You have a phone call."

Chapter Eighteen

Master

"Get out," I growl at the interrupting servant, hunching over my little wolf's body to hide him from sight. *I'm* the only one who gets to see him like this, who gets to enjoy his body blissed out from pleasure. *I'm* the only one who gets to admire his luminous skin and perfect pink cock. The servant stumbles over an apology as he backs out, but the perfect, precarious moment has been ruined.

Eryn is pale, shaking below me, the interruption clearly dragging him from the blissed out place he'd just been in—subspace, or nearly. That something so precious had been shattered so quickly drove my anger even higher, but I know I can't let myself give in to it.

Instead, I slip my finger carefully out of his tight heat, massaging the slightly loosened pucker for several seconds, knowing the emptiness would likely feel strange to someone as inexperienced as he was. Then, I lean down, dropping a kiss to his bellybutton, licking a drop of cum I'd missed back into my mouth. I trail my kisses higher until I reach his neck. I feel no urge to bite, so instead, I suck the skin until a bruise blossoms, a bright mark of ownership on his pale skin. Finally, I take his lips, tasting myself on them.

He parts to my demand, letting my tongue scoop my own flavor from his for several seconds before I break away. "You, my sweet boy, are perfect."

His skin turns a pretty shade of pink, and he drops his focus, not disagreeing but clearly uncomfortable. I'll just have to compliment him more until he believes me. I can't have my little wolf doubting his worth.

He's more than earned every penny I paid for him.

He seems distracted as I tug him to his feet, inspecting his knees for bruising — there is a little — and his back for rug burn — more than a little. My little wolf is a tiger in the sack, squirming and arching so prettily for me.

I think about taking him back to his room for a nap, but I can't. I need him close to me, a feeling too strong to shake — a feeling I haven't allowed myself in decades or longer. A *Bloodbond*, or the start of one, at least.

If I close my eyes, I could see it — the red thread of fate tangling our souls together. Loosely now, easily cut and broken, but capable of weaving tighter into an eternal knot. I've never let one get that far before, but maybe...

I didn't ask for it, didn't plan it...but I can't say I don't want it.

So instead, I lead him upstairs to my bedroom and I tuck the clearly exhausted wolf into *my* bed, beneath *my* covers, where he wraps himself tightly around *my* pillow. Gets his scent all over *my* sheets, and the possessive bastard that I am crows for joy inside.

Mine mine mine mine mine, my inner demon chants over and over like a soundtrack and since I can't argue, I don't bother shutting him up.

He *is* mine, and I'm going to keep him.

* * * *

The phone call I ignored earlier comes back to haunt me several hours later when there's a heavy banging on my front door. Eryn doesn't budge, even when I drag the pillow out from under us and pull it over my face. The knocking finally stops, but only because I hear one of the servants open the door.

A few seconds later, the voice of my best friend — and person I very much want to kill at this exact moment — echoes through the house as Aries hollers up the stairs, "Leviathan, if you don't get your ass out of bed and downstairs, I *will* come up there! And any naked bits I see will be *entirely* your fault!"

I mumble the obvious reply as I roll out of bed and grab my jeans from the floor to tug on. "I'm coming. Hold your kelpies!"

"Too much information, you bastard! Just get down here!" Aries whistles as he walks away from the bottom of the stairs, presumably toward either the parlor or the salon. It's hard to worry about tracking his footsteps when Eryn is blinking his pretty blue eyes up at me.

"What time is it?" he asks around a yawn.

"Not too late," I answer, reaching out to push his pale hair behind his ears so I can see more of his face. "Why don't you go into my bathroom and take a nice long bath? I'll go see what the asshole wants and check on your suit."

"'Kay," he agrees and slides off the bed, the sheets pooling around his hips before he stands. He stretches his arms over his head, the muscles in his back tightening under his skin, highlighting his slender frame. My eyes follow the line of his spine to the dimples at its base, then catch on his ass, a perfect handful, tight and round. I want to bury my face between his cheeks, open him with my tongue, but I don't think he's ready for that yet.

Maybe after I deal with Aries.

Aries is in my parlor, sipping coffee out of a teacup in the pink armchair. His chin is shadowed with the growth of a three-day beard, his eyes ringed with lack-of-sleep bruises. He glares at me when I enter, giving a surly *harumph*.

"Someone's grouchy. I've got extra room if you'd like to take a nap," I tease as I drop into the opposite armchair. "I can even find you a sippy cup." Several actually, bought years ago but put away after everything that happened with Puck.

"Don't Daddy me. You'll only be disappointed," Aries snaps before burying his face in his teacup again. The fine china looks like a toy in his large hand.

"Oh, I always am with you, Aries. What are even doing with your life? Running around with those hooligans. Your mother and I are so disappointed." I shake my head and *tsk*, then duck out of the way of the throw pillow whose purpose he took too seriously.

"I'm actually here on business, Leviathan," he says sternly, his nose in the air.

"I see. Never just for a chat." Not that I'm surprised. I prop my ankle on my knee, waving for him to go on.

"We need you back in Old York."

"Pass," I answer immediately. I'm not ready to leave my new pet. I rarely get possessive, but when I do, there's no use fighting it. My inner demon has claimed him, and I couldn't leave, even if I wanted to — not until the beast is satisfied and the Bloodbond complete. And only if I'm careful not to let it grow into a Soulbond. I've never been tempted before, but now, with Eryn, I fear I won't be able to stop myself.

"Levi. Leviathan. *Friend.*" Aries stretches the last word. "I'm not asking. This isn't a question, or…or a friendly visit. This is an official mandate from the Bureau. You have seventy-two hours to appear at headquarters or your residency permit will be revoked indefinitely."

I scoff and slouch back. "They won't do that. They need me too much."

"Which is exactly why they *will*, Levi. Someone opened another portal, a big one." Aries sets his teacup on the end table and leans forward, elbows on his knees.

"What happened to the wixxes?" When I left nine days ago, they had a whole coven monitoring the city. Surely they should have been able to handle locking down whatever stray practitioner is doing this. There are only so many places in the city suitable for casting circles.

"Whoever it was, they were able to slip by some of our finest and cast the septagram before anyone noticed. By the time the spell tripped the wards, they were already gone. That's why we need you." Aries laces his fingers together at the entreaty.

"I can't help much with a caster. You know magic isn't my strong suit anymore. I'm really only helpful in a reactive sense." Back when I had my *Focus*, maybe I could have been more assistance, but while my magic, unlike a wix's, is limitless, I don't have any natural ability to tap it. I need sigils and potions and a good deal of luck just to light a candle in the wrong weather.

"They brought through a Whisper."

"Shit," I curse and sit forward, brushing my knees against the coffee table. A level three won't die as easily as the pit demons, and Whispers are hard to track. "I really want to help, Aries, but I can't right now." My skin heats as I realize that I'll have to explain. There's no getting out of it. "My demon has claimed the little wolf. I can't leave him this early in the Bonding." Already, my skin itches from the distance, and we're only separated by a single floor.

Once the Bonding is finished, I'll be less possessive, and spending time away from him then might help weaken it. After a year or so, he'll be able to leave my side if he wishes, so by the time his contract is up, it shouldn't be a problem. I'll always be able to find him. My other bonded ones had died in the years since we'd parted, most of old age.

"Bad timing," Aries agrees, his face twisting, but clearly it hasn't changed his mind. "Bring him if you have to, but I can't talk your way out of the consequences if you don't show."

The last thing I want is to bring Eryn into a city plagued by demons, but losing my permanent residency would mean monthly check-ins, frequent home inspections and at least an annual trip back to Kur to file out new visa paperwork. And it's not like I can bring the little wolf with me *there*.

"Fine, I'll be there, but don't think I'm not bringing him, so make sure the Bureau sets me up with better accommodation than last time," I begrudgingly agree.

"It was a four-star hotel," Aries grumbles.

"It didn't have a pool."

"You don't like to swim," he reminds me, as if I don't know that.

"Maybe I want to start."

"You don't. Seventy-two hours, Levi." Aries leaves me pouting, grabbing his coat off the corner of the bookshelf by the parlor door as he departs.

"Fuck." Swiping my hand through my hair as I curse, I realize just how much work it will be to get not only me but my little wolf to Old York. Besides packing, I'll need to arrange the flight details, cancel my reservations for this evening and all manner of boring things I'd rather not concentrate on. I'll make Maggie handle it, I decide, perking up at the thought.

"Maggie!" I holler.

Maybe this won't be so bad after all.

Chapter Nineteen

Pet

"This is horrible," I moan into the puke bag Master kindly passed me at the first sign of my retching. It's still empty, but I doubt it will stay that way much longer. Wolves aren't meant to fly. If we were, we'd have wings.

No wings, so definitely *not* meant to be flying thousands of feet above the ground in a tin can with an honest-to-gods *person* manning the controls. Couldn't Master have booked us a regular flight with a computer piloting it? I trust lines of code so much more than a Blank with a drinking problem.

Which is information I could have done without, but it's not my fault the pilot came out to greet Master before takeoff and all I could smell was cheap whiskey. And not just on his breath... He reeked of it. He was literally sweating it out, staining his white pilot's jacket.

"I thought you'd like the view," Master says contritely, rubbing my back. I'm sure the view is fine, considering the richness surrounding me. The private jet is a far cry from the cramped seating I expected.

"Please don't talk about it," I plead, gagging into the puke bag again. I don't need the reminder of how high up we are. I've never been on a plane before, and after this, I hope I never will be again.

Then I remember that eventually, we'll have to go back to Master's estate and the realization makes me want to cry.

"Are we there yet?" I ask, my voice plaintive.

"Not quite, baby. A bit closer than the last time you asked, though." If he's really as amused as he sounds, I'm going to hit him, consequences be damned. Instead, I make a face that I think is hidden, until he laughs.

Apparently not.

"We're going to die." I don't care how overdramatic he thinks I am. It's a perfectly reasonable fear.

"Baby, I wouldn't let that happen." Master rubs my back, his palm hot against my clammy skin, even through the thin T-shirt. "If the plane *did* crash, which it won't," he hurries to add as I shudder, "I promise I would get you safely to the ground."

Yeah, right, I think, and the disbelief must be written on my face because he chuckles and tugs me out of my seat and onto his lap. With a bit of maneuvering, he has me straddling him, my face tucked close to his neck.

"How about I give you something else to think about, hmm?" He purrs, and before I can answer, he slips his fingers under the waistband of the black trousers he'd dressed me in this morning.

Immediately, I suck in my stomach to give him more room to play. My voice is breathy as I say, "If you think that will help, Master…"

"Such a good little wolf." Then, he curls his fingers around my already stiff dick, and I'm not thinking of anything except the feel of his hand. Three strokes and I'm leaking for him. He gathers my pre-cum in his palm and uses it to coat my erection. Flying? The only one flying now is me.

"Such a good boy," he repeats, his voice almost a growl, deep in his throat. I feel it rumble against my still buried face.

It drags a whimper from my chest, and I smother it by pressing my lips to the skin beneath his ear. I fight the urge to bite, to sink my teeth into his skin as I rut into his hand like an animal. He tilts his neck for me, and the need grows stronger, a foreign feeling that starts as a flutter but soon is like an earthquake under my skin.

He twists his wrist, and it sends lightning through me, but it's not enough. I need...something else. "Please, Master," I beg.

"Tell me what you need, baby." He keeps his hand moving, too slow to push me over but tight enough to keep me on edge.

"More, please, Master." I don't know exactly. *More pressure? More speed?* My hole clenches around nothing as I rut into his hand. "I need..." Something. I want to bite him, claim him in a mate mark, but I can't fathom the thought of hurting my Master, my Alpha.

"I think I know what you need, baby." He lets go of my dick, and I cry out at the abandonment, thrusting into nothing. Before I can complain, he slides his hand out of my pants and grips my hips, lifting me out of his lap and down onto the carpeted floor in the center of the wide walkway.

Then, he strips me quickly. The plane is chilly, but that's not why my nipples immediately form little pink beads on my chest, nor is it the reason I shiver. It's because of the way he looks at me, his eyes devouring me like a starving man. For the first time since he bought me, I find myself willingly tipping the neck, exposing my veins to his mouth if he wishes.

His shadow falls over me as he leans forward, latching his lips to my skin, though he doesn't bite. He presses his tongue against my pulse before dipping lower, into the hollow of my throat, then down my smooth chest. He flicks one nipple then the other, until my hips are pumping forward into air and my cheeks are damp with tears, not from pain but from want.

He caresses my thighs before he forces them open, sitting back abruptly. My dick twitches against my belly. "Look at you, Pet. So hard, leaking just for me." He captures the bead of pre-cum at my tip with his thumb and lifts it to his lips, and that only makes me leak more.

He cups his hand over his suit pants, the fabric straining against his erection, highlighting its girth and length. I can see the dampness where his pre-cum leaves a print on the expensive trousers. It makes me want to press my face against it, make it wetter with my tongue.

I can't help it. I reach for my shaft, but my hand barely touches it when he swats it away. "Did I say you could touch *my* dick?" Master asks, and though his voice is a growl, his lips are a playful grin, and I shake my head. "If you want to come," he says, "you'll do it without touching."

"Master?" I protest, my hips arching off the carpet, "Please, I can't. I need it, please..." My shaft is red and angry looking, and even as close as I am now, just from him *looking* at me like that, I don't think I can spill hands-free.

"You can... I know you can." Master coos as he flicks open his belt, leaving it threaded through the belt loops while he works on the button. His zipper lowers achingly slow while he fishes out his erection.

He drags the tip of it over my inner thighs, painting me with his pre-cum until I'm sticky and shuddering. Then, he shoves my legs flat beneath him so he can straddle them, resting his heavy cock beside mine, nestled into the line of my hip. It dwarfs mine, but rather than shamed, it leaves me feeling small, protected.

Like I don't have to be strong, because he's stronger.

"Look at you, baby." And he *is* looking, his expression dark and hungry. "Perfect," he murmurs, so quietly that I wonder if I'm supposed to hear it.

"You're so big, Master." I want him, either weighing down my tongue or filling the aching emptiness just inches from where he's teasing me.

He shifts off my thighs as if he'd read my mind, slowly but inexorably pushing them toward my chest, until my hips arch off the carpet and I'm open, exposed.

His dick slides from my groin as he tilts his hips, the blunt head dragging over my hole. I cry out at the feeling, the tease. "There, Master, *please.*"

"Mm, you want me to fuck you, baby?" Master rolls his hips against me, his crown massaging my hole with each shift, and I don't even care that it'll hurt, that it's dry. I want it in me. "Want me to shove my big dick into your tight little hole?" It's cheesy, bad porn dialogue at best, but in the moment, it sounds so hot that I can't help the moan that pierces the otherwise-quiet cabin.

"Please, *please*, Master," I'm a broken record, but it's the best my brain can come up with.

"Don't move," he orders, then his weight leaves me while he stretches toward the table a few feet away. He yanks on the drawer and fishes around inside, pulling out a small glass bottle of lube.

A part of me wonders who else he's fucked on this plane, but the larger part shushes it into silence. I don't want jealousy to pull me from the moment. Not even the turbulence shaking the plane can distract me from wanting his dick inside me right *now.*

"Hold your knees back, little wolf," Master orders, so I grab them, keeping myself open for him. He twists open the lube and coats his fingers. "You're so pretty here, baby," Master murmurs, swirling his index finger around my hole.

I clench instinctively as he slowly presses inward, but he doesn't stop until his knuckle brushes against skin. "There you go, baby, such a good boy. So tight for Daddy. I can't wait to get in here. You going to let me in, baby?" He rambles a litany of praise as he slowly works me open with one finger, then two, then three, until I'm a squirming, writhing mess and my stomach is covered with pre-cum from my leaking dick.

It's the second time he's called himself Daddy during sex, a part of me notices, but I put it away for later. My hips are rocking up to meet his fingers, and though three fingers are a painful stretch, it's not enough. I need more.

"Please, I'm ready," I gasp as he immediately drags the tips of his fingers over a spot inside me that sends fireworks straight to the tip of my dick.

"It's going to hurt," Master cautions. "Can you take one more for me?"

I shake my head, knowing one more will either kill me or tip me over, and I don't want to spill without him inside me. "No, now, *please,* Master, *now...*"

He groans like my words are torturing him but yanks his fingers free. I'm achingly empty but only for a second, then the blunt tip of his dick is pressing against my hole, big enough to feel like a fist. I know I can't take it, I can't, but then, with a painful pop, my ass lets him in.

The sound that comes out of me is a mix between a scream and a keen, my entire spine arching off the carpet, but he doesn't move yet, letting me get used to his size. Just the head inside and still I feel like surely I can't take any more.

Then the burn lessens, and his stillness is more punishment than help. My back presses into the carpet as I try to work my hips around him. He just laughs and plants his hand against my lower belly, pinning me down, keeping me still. "You'll take what I give you, baby, and not an inch more."

Sucking in a breath, I decide to take a chance, risk that hearing the word, *that* word, the one that makes butterflies in my stomach each time it slips accidentally from his lips, will make him lose control. "Please, Daddy, I want it all."

He freezes, then a deep groan tears from his throat and he jerks, piercing me with his dick until his hips are flush against my ass. We cry out together at the feeling as I clench around him.

"Say it again," he growls as he rolls his hips, his dick circling in my hole until it rubs insistently against my spot.

"Daddy," I say between ragged breaths, watching the way mouth parts on a gasp. "I want it all, Daddy."

The iron grip he'd held on his control disappears and now he's fucking me, crashing his hips into mine and it hurts, but in the best way, knowing I'm the reason he's losing it, knowing I did that.

He drops down, bracketing my head with his hands, his face above mine so our breath can mingle. My knees are pinned between our chests, and it makes my hips tilt up, so every thrust has him dragging against my spot until I can't do anything but *feel*. Then, he rolls his hips, and the tip of my dick brushes his abs.

It's just enough friction to tip me over and I cry out, spilling into the gap between us, my ass clamping down tight with each spasm. It must be enough for him, as well, because his smooth motion stutters then he cries out, dropping his forehead down onto mine. Heat floods me as he marks my body from the inside.

Several strands of dark hair fall from the band at Master's neck, like a curtain around our faces, and all I can see is him, his eyes squeezed tight, his teeth bared. It should be scary, fangs on display, jaw clenched, but it's not. If he bit me now, I think it would only send me higher.

His whole body shudders and he rocks into me one last time. My ass is sore, but it doesn't stop me from squeezing him, an aborted attempt to keep him inside me, even though he is already pulling out.

Master gives a heavy sigh and sits up, just the head of his shaft plugging my hole. His hands are gentle when he lowers my knees, until my thighs are resting on top of his. My heaving chest is even more obvious as I try to catch my breath. Sweat and cum mix on my skin.

I don't think it can get any hotter, but then Master cups my balls in his hand and lifts them, staring at the place we're still joined. My cock gives a half-hearted spasm, trying to get hard again.

It makes his lips curve into a smirk. "I want to live in you, baby."

My teeth catch my lip and I bite down my moan, unable to hold it in when he shifts, and it sends his not-quite-soft erection back into my body.

"I want to plug you with my cum. Keep you stretched and ready for my *dick*." He keeps talking, but all my attention is on the small, gentle thrusts he's making, like he's pushing his seed back into me, stirring it around with his shaft, making sure he has marked every inch of me he can.

I never want him to leave my body.

Then he brushes against my over-sensitive prostate, and my whole body jerks, accidentally swallowing his dick back in to the root, and if I wasn't hard before, I am again now.

"You like that, baby? Want Daddy to keep you stretched and ready all the time?" The next thrust is intentional. "Can you come again? I want to feel you strangling my cock."

I shake my head but then he curls his hand around my sensitive penis, and I cry out, changing my mind. He wraps his other hand around my neck over his collar and that's it. My shaft spurts again, a much smaller amount, but it feels like so much more, and I'm so sensitive I don't think I can bear it.

But he doesn't let go, holding my soft cock in his palm as he takes me again, fucking into my body until he fills me a second time.

I'm so wrapped up in him that I don't even notice the plane landing.

Chapter Twenty

Master

Eryn is a blissed-out mess beneath me, my dick still lodged in his ass, enjoying the aftershocks of his orgasm as he clenches around me. He's taken two loads of my cum, and it spills out around my cock as it finally softens, reluctantly slipping out.

I can't help it. I scoop the pearly liquid up with my thumb and push it back into his hole, still gaping but already trying to tighten up again. It swallows me like he, too, wants to keep me inside forever.

"Such a good boy," I murmur, dropping onto my stomach for better access. Slowly, almost methodically, I work my tongue over his abs and chest, taking each drop of his cum into my mouth. It seems to relax him, the small shudders of his muscles calming, his breathing returning to normal.

At least until I grip the backs of his thighs and force his knees to his chest again so I can fasten my lips to his hole and clean him of *my* cum. He cries out and tries to squirm free of my hands, my mouth, but I refuse to release my grip. A particularly strong wiggle has me releasing his thighs with one hand to snake it over his hips instead, pinning him down.

It leaves him free to clamp his legs around my head, but I don't mind. He might be strong, but he's not strong enough to hurt me. I lick and suck each drop that tries to escape, and by the time I'm finished, I swear he comes again, though it shouldn't be possible.

I let his legs fall back to the carpet and slide up his body to steal his lips, sharing the flavor of *us* with him. He pants against my mouth. "You are so fucking perfect," I say, kissing him again, unable to resist.

Unfortunately, I know we can't stay forever, since the plane landed sometime between the first and second orgasm and only the courtesy of the flight staff has allowed us the continued privacy.

He opens his mouth to speak but only a groan emerges. I know I've worn him out, but at least he stopped worrying about the flight. I grab his clothes and help him dress, pulling his T-shirt over his head before I pick up his shoes, which he hasn't worn since the flight took off, and slip them onto his feet. I don't know where his socks ended up, but he won't need them. The trip from the airport to the hotel will be short, then he'll be naked again.

And stay that way until I can take him out—which unfortunately will be longer than I like, since I have to visit the latest crime scene first.

It takes me only a few seconds to do up my pants and belt, then I help him onto his feet. He blinks for a second, clearly confused. "We landed?"

I can't help the small laugh that escapes. "Yes, Pet. Safe and sound."

His skin flushes a pretty pink, and I have to remind myself that I can't take him again. Even if we had time—which based on the number of times my phone has buzzed, we don't—his hole was puffy and red when I rimmed him, too sore for another round this quick.

Instead, I tuck him under my arm, preemptively shielding him from the chaos we're likely to meet on the tarmac. With the closure of dozens of airlines, nearly all flights are routed through City Air now. Not only is the airport extremely crowded, but it's packed mostly with Blanks.

Which never fails to cause problems, because guaranteed at least *some* of them are a part of HF, or Humans First. I can ignore their signs and screeching protests, but I don't know if Eryn has ever seen them before.

As I expect, we've barely stepped on the stairs when the hollering of protesters increases. It's not directed at us, since my plane is unmarked, virtually identical to most of the others. Instead, the protesters stand pressed against the chain link fence that separates the tarmac from the public, waving signs and screaming toward the bright blue plane with *SuperAir* on the side.

It is one of the few flights that caters only to Supernaturals, mainly to creatures who, for one reason or another, can't be near Blanks for extended periods of time, like Kelpies, newly turned vampires and Ankhubans—ones who are as likely to kill a Blank as share space.

That doesn't stop the Blanks from screaming about discrimination, though, even though they still haven't managed to even live peacefully with each other.

The last thing anyone needed was a crying baby beside a troll who might think it a snack.

"Ignore them," I mutter to Eryn, who's cringing into my side, his face ducked behind the shield of his blond hair like it will hide him from sight. At least my work with the BAA lets us slip quickly through security and also ensures a car is waiting for us by the sidewalk, our luggage already loaded into the trunk.

We are inside and on the road before any of the HF protestors — or as most of their opponents call them, *Heffers* — notice us.

Eryn stays tucked against my side for the first few minutes but slowly, he peeks out, darting his focus to the window for longer and longer increments until, finally, he is pressed against the glass, his eyes wide. "Everything is so *big*," he exclaims.

I *might* have texted instructions to the driver earlier to take the long way to the hotel, but only because I wanted him to be able to see the city a bit before I need to lock him in the hotel room. A few extra minutes won't kill the BAA.

"That building there? It used to be a cathedral." I point to the old stone building, whose rose window is still in place over the main door. It looks much the same, except for the gargoyles atop the arches. "Now it's the home of the Grand Coven. It caused quite a stir back in the day."

"What about that?" Eryn jabs his finger against the glass a few minutes later, his wince the only sign that it might have hurt.

"Hmm? Oh, that's a hotel, been one for ages. But that?" I lean over his shoulder to point out the building beside it, "That used to be a museum. Now it's a med lab."

He frowns at the glass and brick building. "Really?"

I laugh. "No, it's still a museum. I couldn't resist pulling your leg. But most of the antiques are kept locked away now. They mostly show holos."

The look Eryn gives me is full of offense at the tease, and I can't help ruffling his hair, smiling when he leans into the touch. Unfortunately, we pull up in front of the hotel before I'm ready to stop touching him.

The driver opens the door, and I scoot out, holding out my hand for Eryn to follow, leading him inside to get checked in while the porter helps unload our bags from the trunk. Then, once I have the keycode for our room, I tug him into the elevator and plaster his chest to mine as the doors close, cupping his ass with my hands.

He gasps into my mouth as I capture his lips, unable to resist rediscovering his taste. "I can't get enough of you," I say between kisses, and by the time the elevator stops on the top floor, his lips are swollen, his eyes hazy with lust.

I walk him backward out of the elevator to the only door in the hallway, blindly keying in the code on the lock until it beeps, and I can shove the door open. Our luggage is already waiting, but I ignore it to kick the door closed behind me, spinning to shove Eryn against it. "You are so fucking addicting."

"Master," Eryn whines plaintively, jerking his hips until his dick brushes mine.

"Daddy," I correct him, giving in to the need inside me. "Call me Daddy."

* * * *

The Blood Demon's Pet

"What's got your panties in a twist?" Aries asks just after dawn the next morning, taking a drag of his ciggy. The smoke trickles from his mouth as he grins.

"Shut up," I snap as I crouch down in the alley to stare at the septagram. Unlike the last circle, these lines are wobbly, like the person who carved them couldn't keep their hand still. Were they second guessing their decision, or was it just too much magic to control?

"How'd your boy like the hotel?" Aries ignores my crankiness and asks anyway.

"Seems to like what he saw of it," I mutter, frowning as I reach down to pinch up a handful of burnt gravel. *Too much power*, I'm guessing. Whoever cast this one channeled more energy than they could handle. "I'd get this ground salted ASAP. These lines are still hot."

"Already on it. Why'd he not see all of it? You were late getting here, so can't be a lack of time. You fucked him, didn't you? Go ahead, tell Uncle Aries all about it."

"If you're horny, go get laid. Don't live vicariously through me. Are they bringing iron stakes? They should bury some at each point to be safe. There's enough power left to summon a lesser demon, if the wrong practitioner stumbles on it." I straighten up and glare at the flattened fence across from me. The Whisper clearly wants me to think it went that way, which means it's the only direction I probably don't have to check. Unless it knew I would think that and went that way anyway.

I hate the fucking smart ones. There's no way of telling how much it knows of earth, and whether it would know of my work with the BAA. I've become somewhat of an urban legend in Kur...or so I've heard.

"Oh, come on. Don't be that way. Just tell me, is he as tight as you hoped he'd be?" Aries whines and something about it stokes a fire in my chest.

He's asked me the same question a hundred times about a hundred different lovers, and I've never cared. Sometimes I even answer, but not this time. This time, it does nothing but piss me off and I snarl, spinning on my best friend with flames in my eyes. "Don't talk about him like that. Don't even *think* about him. He is *mine.*" The last word is more growl than anything.

Aries lifts his hands and takes a step back. "Sure, of course. Just joking around."

I clench my eyes closed and breathe in deeply through my nose, seeking calm. "Sorry," I lie, because I meant every word I said, even if I didn't mean to snap at him like that.

"Well, anyway...the sooner you get done with this"—he waves his hand at the septagram— "the sooner you can get back to your boy, right? We already canvassed the warehouses down that way." He points toward the fence. "So far, nothing."

"You won't find anything," I say, glaring toward the main road in the other direction. There's nothing to go on. Unlike in the park, there's no footprints to follow, since everywhere else in Old York is cement and sidewalk, and the Whisper was smart enough to circle the septagram enough to lay his scent through the whole area. If I were pressed, I'd say it was strongest to the north, but that, too, could be a misdirect.

"That's why we brought you in," Aries oh-so-helpfully points out.

Even if the trail was fresh, I doubt I'd be having better luck. I straighten up and fiddle with the end of my braid. "Nothing on the radios? Unexpected deaths, sightings? Anything?"

"Not a peep."

I curse but I'm not surprised. Unlike the pit demons, who even with orders have the attention span of a squirrel and can't help but cause troubles, Whispers are single-minded. "The other demons ended up near Jackson Heights, yeah?"

"Thereabouts."

"So whatever their master is summoning them for, it's likely near there," I think out loud.

"I'll send some agents that way." Aries pulls out his phone and starts to dial, but I grab his wrist first.

"Make sure they stay under the radar—unmarked cars, no uniforms. If the demon spots them, it'll go underground. I don't know what it's looking for, but that means I don't know how long it can afford to wait. Could be years." And I am *not* spending any longer than I have to with my thumb up my ass in the city, not even with my little wolf to distract me.

Chapter Twenty-One

Pet

The sound of the hotel room door clicking shut jars me from sleep. I jerk up, my heart pounding, and nearly roll off the armchair I'd passed out in. The large room is shadowy and dark, and all I can see at first is a silhouette by the door. I blink and it comes into focus as Master. *Daddy,* my brain corrects.

He drops his duffel bag before pulling off his leather jacket, letting it fall on top. Then, he tucks his hands in his pockets and strolls closer. "Miss me?" he asks once he's standing over me, his white teeth glinting in the low light seeping through the curtains.

"Yes, Daddy," I admit, clenching the arms of the chair to keep myself from springing at him. Already, just the way he is looming over me makes my cock tingle awake, hardening against my thigh. I drag the throw pillow into my lap to hide it.

"Don't be shy, baby. Nothing to be embarrassed about," Master says as he throws the pillow away and grips my knees, dragging me to the edge of the seat until my dick is standing like a flagpole straight into the air. "Look at that, how hard you are for me. Good thing I've got plans for you."

"Plans?" I ask, thrusting my hips pointlessly.

"Mm-hmm. I've made us reservations."

Master might be planning on us going out, but I can't tell from the way he strokes his hands over my thighs.

"Isn't it late?" I ask, guessing from the darkness out of the window rather than a clock.

"Where we're going, it's considered *early*." Master purrs, his voice leaking arousal like my dick is leaking pre-cum. He gives my thighs one last stroke before he steps back. "Let's get you dressed."

"Yes, Daddy," I agree, obediently following him into the bedroom, sitting on the edge of the bed while he goes into the walk-in closet.

What he comes out with looks more like scraps then anything I'd call an *outfit*. A lace jock that barely contains my dick, a pair of white lace shorts so small they're practically a belt and a baggy white button-down shirt that will cover it all. "Don't worry." Master leers as he helps me into them. "You'll only be wearing it for the drive."

As if it not matching is what I'm worried about. My legs look a thousand miles long beneath the hem — a thousand miles of smooth, bare flesh, shaved clean the way Mas…Daddy asked before he left first thing this morning.

Daddy spins me to face the mirror, dancing his hands up my thighs and under the hem of the baggy shirt, showing off the soft lace, a heady contrast to the dick straining the front. If I look at my reflection objectively, I can admit it's hot—sexy, even—but only if I pretend it's not me.

"What do you think, pretty boy? You want me to put you in a pair of heels, make these legs look even longer? Mm, no…I know just the thing. Don't move. I want you to stand here and look at your pretty body in the mirror. Touch yourself like I would, keep yourself hard for me." Daddy puts my hand on my dick, squeezing my fingers with his until I'm jerking myself over the lace while he goes back to the closet.

It's weird at first, staring at myself and trying to stay hard, not wilt at my reflection, but it gets easier when I picture him standing behind me, the way his frame would dwarf mine, my skull barely brushing his chin—his shoulders wider than mine, his hands like dinner plates on my skin. He can almost span my waist with only one of them.

I suck in a breath as I imagine him behind me again, pushing his thick dick into my ass in front of the mirror, lifting my balls out of the way so I can see him spearing into me. I wonder if I could see him pressing against my stomach from the inside, as big as he is.

The lace shorts are sticky when Daddy finally comes out, a wet patch on the front highlighting my arousal. His eyes focus on it and darken, his tongue swiping over his lower lip. He has a pair of black combat boots, just like his but smaller and clearly new, hanging from one hand, pink socks in the other.

"Hands off now, baby." He groans, dropping the boots in front of me. "I want everyone to see how hard you are for me." My dick twitches at the thought, even as nerves bite at my throat. He ignores both, kneeling in front of me and putting the thigh-high socks on each foot, then the boots, lacing them tightly up my calves. He lingers, stroking the leather before clearing his throat. "Perfect."

He straightens and tucks me under his arm to lead me out of the hotel room and into the elevator. My skin is hot at the thought of being out like this, that other people will see me and... And what? I calm a bit as I realize that Daddy's collar does more than show he owns me. I won't get in trouble for this, because Daddy – my master, my *owner* – says it's okay. He told me to wear this, and I have to obey.

The thought calms me, letting me focus on the way Daddy's hands wander a bit through the ride down the elevator. Nothing obscene, just enough to keep me hard and aching.

The driver of the car Daddy hired keeps his face almost pointedly turned forward. The only time I meet his eyes in the rear-view mirror, his skin turns nearly as pink as mine is. I wonder how much Daddy has to pay him for this drive, since motor cars are rare, and people licensed to drive them even rarer. Finding one willing to ignore Daddy's antics had to have been even harder.

"Are you nervous?" Master murmurs in my ear.

I want to lie and say that I'm not, but I can't. My nod is short, stilted and I swallow. I won't get in trouble, but I can't help the fear that I'm going to fail him or worse, disappoint him – or he's going to abandon me again. Every time he's made me soar, I've come crashing back to earth the next day when he disappears.

"Tell Daddy what's wrong, baby," he orders.

"I..." I bite my lips to stem the flow of words long enough for me to think, though it only makes the worry worse. If I say the truth, will he be angry? Will it make him turn the car around and take me back to the hotel, leave me there while he goes out alone?

Do I want that? The thought of him doing to others the things he's done to me makes me angry. I want to be the only one he touches, the only one he kisses. And, strangely, the only one he bites.

Daddy thumbs my lip free from my teeth with a sigh. "None of that, baby. Tell me what's wrong."

"I don't want you to forget about me tomorrow," I finally blurt, unable to resist the pull of his golden eyes.

"Forget about you?" He jerks back slightly, his eyebrows lifting.

My nod is brief. "I...I liked what we did in the garden, when you..." My skin heats but I force myself to keep going. "When you played with me and let me taste you, but then you got so cold. And... And you showed me the wildflowers, and gave me a bath, and let me sleep in your bed, but then you..." I swallow against the lump rising in my throat. "You put me back in that room and you left me."

Dropping my eyes to the leather seating makes it easier to add the last. "Then a few days ago, on the plane... But then you brought me to the hotel and..." I trail off. It hadn't been bad. It's not like I can complain about having free rein of a suite in a fancy hotel, endless things to watch on the holo, food on demand at the press of a button.

"Left you alone," Daddy finishes, his voice sad.

"I know you had to go to work," I hurriedly add. He might like to call me 'baby', but I'm not. I understand that he can't be with me all the time. Just because he owns me, doesn't me he owes me anything.

"But you were lonely." He looks away, and it's easy to read the distress on his face. "Back at home…at the estate," he clarifies, "you're lonely there, too?"

I don't want to answer but refuse to disobey, so I nod, barely more than a tilt of my head. "There's nothing to do. If…if I could have a book or two, maybe…"

"That's not enough," he interrupts. The anger in his voice makes me flinch, but when he meets my eyes, it's clear that it's not directed at me, but at himself. "When we go home, things will change, I promise. I'm not used to… My feeders are normally criminals." He lifts his finger to stroke my unmarked forehead. "Often dangerous ones. Keeping them in the basement—or if they are really good, the blue room—keeps my staff safe and stops them from doing anything to trigger this." He drops his hand to the collar clasped around my throat.

The collar seems to shiver at his touch…or maybe that's me.

But before I can do more than swallow, the driver is pulling the car up to a curb and Master straightens, glancing out of the window. "We're here. But Eryn"—my whole body jerks at the sound of my name on his lips—"I want you to know that you can tell me no to *anything* we do in here, okay?" He scans my face as I nod. "Anything at all. I want to keep you so blissed out I'm the only one you see, but I *don't* want you scared or hurting. Promise you'll say if I go too far."

"Yes, Master," I answer immediately but a shiver betrays my nerves as I wonder what he's going to do to me that he's giving me an out now.

"Daddy," he corrects gently, curling his fingers around the back of my neck to pull me closer, until I'm practically in his lap. "Call me Daddy."

"Yes, Daddy."

* * * *

The building looks plain outside, the red brick façade chipped and dirty, but inside...? Inside is sleek and expensive. The black marble floor is shiny but dotted with soft pillows, which I realize quickly are to kneel on. The first room we enter reminds me of a restaurant but fancier than any I've ever seen on a holo. It's crowded with people, but quiet. A bar sprawls to the left, shadowy booths line the far wall on the right.

I can't see much of the people inside each booth, but from the way the shadows are writhing, I know they are doing more than just eating.

Daddy stands just behind me, his heat betraying how close he is. He lets me look for a few seconds before he leans down to speak softly into my ear. "Go to the bar and order a glass of water for you and a Bloody Mary for me. Don't worry about the tab. They'll know what to do. When you have them, come find me."

Before I can protest, he has stripped the baggy shirt from my chest, leaving me in only my tiny shorts. Then he's gone, off to find us a booth, and I have no choice but to obey.

My heart beats faster the closer I get to the bar. Unless I'd done so as a child with my mother, I've never ordered anything from anyone before—never been in a bar or a restaurant. We don't have them on pack land. I don't know the first thing about getting a bartender's attention, especially in a fancy place like this.

There's three of them, all dressed to the nines — black suits over red shirts, hair perfectly in place. A far cry from my own garb.

Despite the difference, I barely step up before one is in front of me, a woman with sharply pointed ears but a kind smile. "What can I get you, love?"

"Um…" I stutter at first before I manage to say, "A water and a Bloody Mary, please."

Her eyes dart over my shoulder, scanning a second before her grin turns as sharp as her ears. "Ah, here with Prince Leviathan, are you? He hasn't been to play in a while." She turns to prep the drinks, then passes me a glass of water and…what looks suspiciously like blood.

My nose crinkles at the copper scent but I only mutter "Thank you," before I pick them both up, turning to look for the man who owns me. Master is leaning against a booth, gripping the edge of the table behind him, his legs crossed at the ankle. In his suit, he looks dangerous and dark and far too good for me.

But he doesn't take his eyes off me as I cross the floor to stand in front of him. "Good boy. Put the drinks on the table."

I obey quickly. Too quickly, because the water sloshes over the top onto the table. "Sorry!" I cry a bit too loudly, trying to clean the spill with my hand.

Master grabs my wrist, halting the frantic movement, his smile gentle. "It's fine, baby." Keeping his grip on me, he snags a napkin with his other hand and cleans it quickly. Then, he lets me go so he can slide into the booth.

Somehow he makes it look graceful, the process of scooting to the center so his back is to the wall, face outward toward the bar. I shift my weight, not sure

KD Ellis

where he wants me, but then his smile turns sharp. "I want you on your knees."

I drop, hitting hard, my breath coming fast. Kneeling, all I can see is the underside of the table above me and his spread thighs. Then his hand is below the table, finger crooking, beckoning me closer. "Crawl to me, baby."

Skin threatening to burst into flames, I obey, crawling under the table. There's just enough room for me to sit upright if I try. I move forward until I'm between his knees. Hidden under the table but able to see him and for him to see me.

"I have a friend coming to meet me, so you have two choices, baby." Master is looking at me with heat in his eyes and without even knowing what the choices are, I know he likes one of the options better. "You can sit at my feet quietly, like a good little pet, and when we get back to the hotel, I'll take you apart in our bed. Or"—he shifts in his seat and something about his expression pulls me in—"you can take me in your mouth right here, keep my dick nice and warm while I talk to my friend and I'll—"

It's clear before he finishes speaking which one he wants, and I don't need the promise of future pleasure to give it to him. Before he can finish, I free him from his pants and take him into my mouth. Something inside me wants to please him, to be his good little boy—some small seed of trust growing into something else, something I hesitate to name.

He groans, fisting a hand in my hair. "No, don't suck. Just keep me warm. Yes, just like that." He breathes out praise as I immediately stop sucking, just relax my mouth, letting his weight rest on my tongue. I can taste his pre-cum as it drips down my throat.

I stiffen slightly when I hear a set of footsteps approaching the table, then a friendly voice greeting my master. Daddy pats my hair in a soothing gesture until I relax again.

"Evening, Aries," Daddy says, releasing my hair to take a drink. I pull myself in closer to him as the man sits down, his knees inches away from my skin. Daddy goes back to stroking my hair.

"Levi," the deep-voiced man named Aries says on a sigh. "Thought you were bringing your new pet with you. Change your mind?"

I meet Daddy's eyes. He smirks down at me, then winks. "No, not at all."

"Forget him in one of the back rooms, then?" Aries slouches a bit, which I only notice when his knee brushes my bare side and I tense. There's a moment of silence, then the man leans over, meeting my eyes.

"Well, well, well. You're right, Levi, he does have a pretty blush." The Black man looks amused at my obvious embarrassment, though from the way he adjusts himself in his pants, he clearly likes the view.

"Doesn't he, though," Master agrees. He gives his hips a little thrust. I can't hold back my moan as he shifts in my mouth. It's hard not to suck. I want to feel him fucking my mouth, making it his and *only* his. He just pats my cheek. "He's such a good boy."

"Are you going to play with him tonight?" Aries asks. I try to ignore the weight of his gaze on me. The only thing that matters is Daddy, and Daddy wants my mouth keeping him warm. I breathe through my nose, taking in his smell, the musk that is distinctly him.

"I haven't decided," Daddy admits, and my eyes dart up to meet his. They're warm and I feel like I'm drowning in them. "What do you think, baby? Want me to take you out back and string you up for everyone to see? Turn your pretty ass pink before I fuck it?"

Liquid fire unspools in my stomach and my hips pump uselessly into empty air. I don't let him slip from my mouth, but I have to swallow my moan. My tongue accidentally flicks over the satiny skin of his dick, and he groans.

"I think someone likes that," Daddy finally moves, pumping my mouth until I'm panting around him, but just when I think I'll get to taste him, he grips my hair and pulls me off.

He tucks himself into his pants, even buttoning them closed, then drags me out from under the table and onto his lap. Up here it seems so much brighter, like I'm exposed to everyone, though I know it's all in my head. The light above us is barely more than a flicker.

"Eryn, this is Aries, my annoying friend," Daddy introduces. I stay quiet but give him a little wave. "Now, now, be polite, baby. Say, 'Hello, Mister Aries'."

"Hello, Mister Aries," I finally whisper.

"Hello, Eryn. Your master tells me you've been a good boy for him." Aries' voice has lost most of the mocking tones it had held when he spoke to Daddy. It's almost gentle now.

"I try," I admit. My nerves are growing again now that I'm out from under the table, so I start rolling one of the buttons on Daddy's suit between my fingers.

"And that's why you're a good boy." Master purrs, closing his hand over mine, stilling the fidgety movement. "Would you like to try something else?"

"Daddy?" *Is he going to tie me up now? Will I like it? What if I don't? Will he be angry?* I don't want to disappoint him.

He tips his head toward the floor, clearly a sign for Aries to scoot out because he does, then he follows, setting me on my feet before he stands. I catch our reflection in the mirror across from us and my breath catches. He's taller than I am, broader, but that's not the only difference. The contrast is sharp, with him in his suit, hair pulled back. He looks like a model, or a businessman. Someone important. Me, I look... I drop my eyes. The shorts leave my skinny frame on display.

I know none of the clothes he'd bought me were cheap, but me? I look it.

Daddy tips my face up to his with a frown. "What's going through that pretty little head of yours?"

I shrug, unable to avoid his eyes but not willing to say it out loud, either. If he hasn't realized it yet, that I'm as worthless as Beta always said, I don't want to be the one to tell him. Not yet.

He scans my face before gripping my shoulder, spinning me until I have no choice but to stare into the mirror again, this time with him behind me. "What do you see, baby? Do you see what I do? Because I see someone beautiful and brave. Look."

Slowly, he slides his hand off my shoulder and up, curving long fingers around my neck, over the thin gold collar. "I could have picked anyone at the market to wear this, and I chose you."

I swallow, the collar tightening around my throat at the reminder, but he isn't finished.

"Look," he says, skimming his hand down my chest to the base of my ribs. "See how small you are? Perfect for me to carry." He nips at my ear, and I yelp. "Just the right size to bounce on my dick."

I harden at the thought, the realization that if he wanted, he *could* lift me, impale me on his cock with little effort, move me like a rag doll to fuck himself on.

"And look at this." Daddy moves his hand even lower, cupping my groin, stretching the already tight shorts even more over my erection. "See how hard you get for me? So whatever you're worried about, I want you to let it go. There's just me…and you."

The whimper that I can't hold back makes him laugh, but all he does is pat my dick. "Let's go play."

Chapter Twenty-Two

Daddy

Whatever insecurity had overcome my boy in the lounge seems to flee as we step into the playrooms. Either he's really past it or the newness of everything just makes him forget. I'm inclined to think it's the latter.

The playrooms here at Syren are some of my favorites to play in. They have a little bit of something for everyone, from restraints and harnesses, inversion tables and pillories and whipping benches all the way to cribs and wet rooms.

Eryn can't seem to figure out what to look at. At first, his gaze is glued to the floor, but he glances up every few seconds. I stay quiet, letting him look, watching what *he* watches. I had a plan when I brought him here, a plan involving a bit of public kneeling, maybe a blowjob, but that changes as I watch him.

His gaze keeps returning, as if inevitably, to the same couple. I don't know them, but I admire their physique, noticing the similarities between them and us. The larger man is wearing leather pants and nothing else. The boy at his feet is small, like Eryn, though his skin is copper, and his ears are pointed.

He's wearing a blindfold, hands bound in front of him, resting on his thighs. His Dom circles behind him with a leather crop, pausing to run the tongue along the boy's shoulders. He teases for a second before striking, and though we're too far away to hear, Eryn still flinches as it lands.

"You like watching them, Pet?" I ask.

Eryn bites his lip but nods.

"Why?" I press when he doesn't say anything else, just stares. My little wolf flushes and drops his gaze to the floor, his only answer a subtle shift of his shoulder.

"Is it their size difference? Do you like how powerless the boy looks on his knees?"

Twin spots of red flare on Eryn's cheek as he jerks his head.

"Would you like to be on your knees like that in front of me, where everyone can see you? Let them watch you give yourself over?"

He nods again, and the red spreads along his cheekbones.

I trace the blush with my fingers. "Do you think he likes that we can see him, but he can't see us? The only thing he can do is wait and *feel*? Take what his master gives him, when he gives it?"

Eryn's moan is sudden, and louder than I expect, and now I know what I'm going to do. I grip his elbow and pull him farther into the dark-red-lit room, leading him to a semi-secluded area of the playroom. He goes to his knees easily when I point.

Nudging his thighs a bit farther apart with my shoe puts him in the position I want, then I stand over him, waiting until he looks up at me to work my tie loose. The silk is good for more than just appearance. I wrap it loosely around the palm of my hand, running the tail over his skin, enjoying the goosebumps that follow.

"I'm going to blindfold you," I say as I move behind him, enjoying the way his breathing upticks. "All I want you to do is listen and feel." *And taste*, though I keep that to myself. His whole body shudders, his mouth parting on a gasp before he nods quickly, like he thinks I'll stop if he doesn't.

It only takes seconds to wrap the tie around his eyes and blind him. The black silk is a nice contrast to his pale skin. I can't resist carding my fingers through his hair, fisting it at his neck like a handle as I tip his face back...blind and powerless. "Beautiful."

Then, I slide the thumb of my other hand over his lips, dipping in briefly just to tease. The tip of his tongue flicks over it, and I have to wonder though, who of us is teasing whom? I step back, breaking contact.

There's so much I want to do to him here — tie him up and flog him, strip him down and make him dirty. But I don't want to push him too far, don't want to break him. The red thread binding us together tightens. I feel it thrumming.

Get him dirty, though... I can do that.

I drag my zipper down slowly, knowing he can hear it, and his moan proves it. A single button is the only thing that separates my dick from his mouth, and it's the easiest thing in the world to pop it open. The blindfold only draws attention to his lips, full and pink and wet from his tongue.

Rubbing the crown over his lips leaves them shiny with pre-cum, and when he licks them clean, my dick twitches in my hand. "Oh, baby, you don't even know what you do to me. Open your mouth, little wolf."

He does immediately, and his obedience is a heady thing. Instead of my dick, which I know he expects, I slip two fingers into his mouth, pressing on his tongue with the pads of my fingers.

Exploring the shape of his mouth, the hardness of his teeth, knowing he could bite down at any moment but knowing also that he won't, that nothing but my words, my order, keeps him still and in place, his mouth open.

He whines when I run a knuckle over his hard palate, slowly stroking the ridges but doesn't bite down, doesn't do anything but keep...his...mouth... open. *Obedient.* My fingers are sopping when I draw them free. Perfect for when I tug down his shorts and wrap my hand around his dick. It's hot against my palm and he cries out, even though I don't stroke, just grip.

"Mouth open," I remind him when it threatens to close. Immediately, he obeys. I straighten back up, and this time, it's not my fingers that I press into his mouth. It's my dick. Just the head at first, and I wonder what he'll do.

Will he try to suck, natural urges overcoming my order? Instead, his lips stay parted though a keen spills from his throat, his breath tickling my dick.

I don't move, torturing myself as much as him, until his tongue twitches and the feel of it skimming over the underside of my dick breaks my control. "Good boy. *Now* you can suck."

And with his talented mouth, it doesn't take long for me to paint his throat.

* * * *

Pet

The horizon is pink when Daddy helps me out of the car outside our hotel. He lets me lean against him as we take the elevator up to our floor, and when I can't get my fingers to work, he helps me get undressed, even pulling one of his shirts over my head. It hangs to my knees but makes me feel like he's holding me in his arms, even when he lets me go to grab my toothbrush from the bathroom.

He brings it out to me with toothpaste preloaded and helps me brush, even holding a cup for me to spit in. "Good boy," he says, so quietly that I almost miss it. "Sit on the bed for me while I take care of these."

Sitting on the bed, my legs swinging over the edge, heels hitting the mattress, I struggle to stay sitting up. My body feels boneless, weightless, like I'm floating. But some part of me must still be tuned in to Daddy because when he comes out of the bathroom, I immediately perk up, searching him out. After spending most of the night blindfolded, only able to feel as he fucked my mouth, then bent me over something hard and unyielding to take my ass, teased me with something soft then something prickly, made me hear and smell and taste and *feel* but not *see*... Now, all I want to do is stare.

I don't know what he sees when he looks at me, but he smiles as he approaches. "Go ahead and lie back, baby. Let me tuck you in."

I lie back, my gaze still on his, and he pulls the blanket up. His fingers are gentle as he shifts the pillow under my head. "Sleep, baby. I'll be here when you wake up, I promise."

Chapter Twenty-Three

Daddy

I don't know what time it is when my phone rings, and I don't particularly care. My little wolf is still sleeping and that means it's too early. It goes quiet but when it starts ringing again, I sigh and roll out of bed, fishing my phone from the pocket of last night's pants.

Aries's name flashes across the screen just before I answer. "What?"

"Need you...at the...American...Museum of... Natural History," he says between pants, clearly out of breath. "The Whisper...is here."

"Shit," I curse, glancing at Eryn, still sleeping. I promised I would be here when he woke up, but I can't leave a level three demon running amok, just to keep my word. Shaking Eryn awake makes guilt rise, but there's nothing I can do.

He blinks his pretty eyes open at me, his sleepy smile fading quickly when he sees the phone still at my ear. But all he says is, "You have to go?"

"I'm sorry." I grab him by the neck and drag him in to steal a kiss before I shove the phone at him. "Listen for me, tell me what he says."

As he relays the information Aries gives him — silent alarm tripped, Demon wards broken, nothing missing but Whisper still on sight — I pull on my gear, lacing my boots up last. I snag the phone back and bark "Five minutes," into the mouthpiece before shoving it in my pocket.

"I'm so sorry, baby. I gotta go. I promise —" I start saying.

"Go. I understand," Eryn smiles, and while it looks sad, I see a strength shining even brighter. If I had a heart, a piece of it would have broken as I left the room, staying behind with my little wolf.

I'd kept the letter of the promise I'd made him last night, not leaving before he woke, but not the spirit. I know it had to have been hard for him to admit his worries in the car, the fear of abandonment, and here I am, abandoning him again.

Not that I have a choice — not a good one, anyway.

A car would take too long, so on the sidewalk, I reach down into my core, where my magic stays furled tight. It's wild and unruly, even sleeping, so all it takes is a little poke. It wakes with a fiery snarl and consumes my mortal body, leaving only energy in its place.

Energy is fast.

Energy is fluid.

It lets me flow from the hotel to the museum in seconds, panicked screams following me, though I move too fast for them to linger. It takes me longer to reform my body than it did to travel. My sword is barely formed in my hands when I see the Whisper.

It isn't frightening, not if you don't know what it is. The size of a small child, it wouldn't look out of place in a schoolyard. I'm sure when it walked into the museum, the only question anyone asked was where its mommy was.

Until it opened its mouth.

Now, its jaw is unhinged, hundreds of coal-black teeth sprouting from it like broken glass. Blood, likely from the security guard dead near the door, dries on its chin and neck. At least the museum is by now empty but for the bodies. It begs the question, though, of where Aries ended up.

I don't have time to worry. The Whisper lets out a shrill screech, sharp and piercing. The glass display cases aren't the only things that shatters. I feel my eardrums rupture like overfilled balloons. The pain is hardly noticeable—a mere scratch compared to the various tortures inflicted on me over the centuries—but the inky blood trickling down my ear canal is an itchy distraction.

The demon takes advantage of my momentary head twitch to lunge, covering the span of feet between us in seconds. I dodge, but its teeth snap close enough for me to feel the draft.

Backing away means giving up ground, but it also gives me precious seconds to plan my attack...and to notice its pained, shifting eyes. It doesn't want to be here. Unfortunately for both of us, a demon obeying a binding is put down the same as a free one. So I lift my sword again and stop my retreat.

"Come on, then. Come and get me."

* * * *

"Damn it, if you'd kept your men out of here for another forty seconds, I'd have had it," I snarl at Aries, wiping the blood from my face with a towel I suspected was meant to clean off the artwork.

"Well, how was I supposed to know you were luring it into a trap? It certainly *looked* like it was about to eat your face off!" Aries snaps back, glaring at the broken skylight his elite team of Venators had rappelled through, then at the shattered window the Whisper had fled through when the sound had pulled my attention away for the span of a second.

"And while it was busy chewing, I was going to stab it in the blood sack." It's the only surefire way to kill a Whisper, since they could regenerate from pretty much anything else.

Aries looks queasy, but it's not like I can't fix any damage the Whisper would have caused. A simple dissolution to energy and back, and I'd be good as new. Now, we are right back where we started, with the Whisper loose and nowhere to look.

At least now, we have a lead. "Whatever it wanted is still here. It didn't take anything with it," I point out as I wipe the blood from my sword and sheathe it.

"Unless whatever it was looking for here was never here in the first place," Aries grumbles, eyeing the museum cases with a grimace. "Do you know how many artifacts this museum has, Levi? It'll take us days just to go through the catalog." It is one of the only museums in the country that still displays actual relics.

"Good thing you have people for that, and since I'm not one of them…" I give my fingers a waggle and walk away, glass crunching under the soles of my boots.

"Call me if you find anything interesting…or don't." A shrug and I'm out of the door, hailing a cab I have every intention of making the Bureau pay for.

It's only a ten-minute drive but it feels like longer and I take the stairs two at a time rather than waiting for the elevator. I want my boy, need to see that he's safe, though I have no reason but for the niggling worry in the back of my mind to suspect he isn't.

Eryn must have left the bed to shower at some point because his hair is damp where it spreads across the sheets. He's curled around my pillow when I, still dusty and covered in blood, come into the bedroom. I should wait, strip my gear and shower first, but instead I crawl right into bed, unable to resist gathering him into my arms.

Especially when the covers shift and I realize he's still naked.

Hunger stirred up from my fight with the Whisper makes me long to sink my teeth into his neck, but his reaction from the last time he woke with me inside him makes me hesitate. I'm not used to hesitating.

Maybe he'll like waking up inside of me better.

Sneaking under the covers is easy, taking his soft cock into my mouth even easier.

It doesn't take long for him to thicken and grow until he fills my mouth, butting against my throat. When I swallow around his crown, his hips jerk under my hands, and even though he's not yet awake, he whimpers and gasps.

I can tell when he wakes because his body stills, freezing up like a statue. When I look up, his eyes are wide and locked on me. "Daddy," he gasps, cheeks pink. "What are you doing?"

"Tasting you, baby," I pull off just long enough to say, wrapping my hand around his dick instead. "Then I want to *taste* you."

I can tell he knows what I mean from the way he bites his lip, but he nods, a small fragile thing. It's enough to encourage me into taking him back into my mouth again, coaxing him to the heights of his climax and shoving him over until his seed, salty and bitter, coats my throat.

"Delicious." I purr as I let his softening dick fall, sated, against his belly. Like a cat on the prowl, I creep back up his body, dragging my own heavy cock, still bound in bloody leathers, over his skin, my eyes fixed on his neck, on the way his throat moves when he swallows—more importantly, the way his pulse dances under his ear.

His body recognizes me. I see it in the way his head tips to the side, veins exposed in offering. One I fully intend to claim and take as mine.

A bead of sweat trails down the column of his throat, and I can't resist catching it with the tip of my tongue and following its path along his flesh. It draws a shiver up through his body that I catch with my fingers and soothe away.

When I finally let my fangs slip under his skin, his only reaction is an indrawn breath he releases in a moan. At first, the riptide of my hunger drags me under, but the tips of his finger digging into my shoulder pulls me back to shore, to safety—for him more than me. Hunger sated, I let my teeth slide free, but my mouth stays latched, flicking my tongue over the wound, gathering the last few drops of his honeysuckle blood before it heals.

Slowly, he lifts his hands from my shoulders and brushes them through my hair. His fingers are hesitant, like he doesn't know if he's allowed to touch me or how much. It makes me grip his wrist and drag it down to press a kiss to the center of his palm. "Did you miss me?" I finally ask, pulling back to meet his gaze.

His cheeks are still pink, but his eyes are glazed as he nods. I worry I stayed under too long, drank too much, until I feel his dick, hard as steel, against my belly. A rock of my hips lines my dick with his and my will to leave the bed and shower dies a little more.

My thighs force his apart, creating space for me to slip my hand between us. A dip of my shoulder lets me prop his knee on my elbow, the stretch exposing his hole to my insistent finger.

"Tell me you missed me, baby, or I'll stop..." My finger circles his entrance, and I feel it flutter at the pressure.

"I missed you, Daddy." His voice breaks when I slide in my finger, crooking it until I find his prostate and massage it. It draws out a keen from his mouth, and I can't wait to swallow the sound. I steal it from his lips in a bruising kiss, coaxing the cry out again. He runs a hand through the dried, cracking blood on my skin. "You're dirty... Oh, don't stop, Daddy, I think...I don't think I care, want you like *this*."

A second finger makes him tense, his hole fluttering around the digits, so I wait patiently for him to relax. "You can take me," I remind him, slowly twisting my wrist. Not thrusting in or out, just massaging the tight ring until it loosens.

"More," he pants, and part of me wants to deny him, tease him longer until he's a sobbing, aching mess. Instead, I give him a third finger. He clenches around it, so tight that my mouth waters. I've sampled his ass already, but it's still just as hot. "Please, please, *please…*" The words spill from his mouth.

I can't deny him after his pretty begging.

A second, then moments later a third finger loosens him just enough I think he can take me. I pop the button on my leathers and let my dick escape. It slaps against his furled pucker, and the monster inside me wants to push in, take him like this, rough and demanding. Instead, I stretch over him to grab the lube off the nightstand and slick myself up. A smooth, steady push and he opens to me, the entrance to his body tight and hot…and made just for me.

I'm the only one who has touched him here. I want to reach inside his body with my fist while I plunge my cock into his mouth, fill every opening he has — touch him in his most sensitive parts.

Make him bleed and consume him so he's always a part of me.

Instead, I make him fly, reining in the desires of the monster only by unleashing the man's.

When I finally wrap my fingers around his dick and let him fuck my palm, he screams, and his warm seed splatters his pale stomach. His whole body shudders, twitches with aftershocks until his muscles go limp. I fuck into him a few more times, jagged thrusts of my hips into his body, until I spend inside him, marking him from the inside out.

Chapter Twenty-Four

Pet

After Master and I shower — or more accurately, after Master showers me, stroking my come-sore body — he dresses me in a surprisingly normal pair of blue jeans and a plain gray pullover. He fiddles with the sleeves, rolling them up over my elbows to bare my forearms. They aren't corded like his, no bulging veins to drool over, but he still trails soft fingers down to my wrists. "Go put on your shoes. The black ones," he clarifies, and of course I obey.

I'll always obey, not just because the wolf inside me, stubborn though he is, has adopted him as our Alpha. I wonder if that's why he's strangely calm, considering how close the Goddess Moon is to her monthly visit. I push the nerves down as I finish lacing my shoes and stand back up.

Master doesn't take my hand. He plants his palm on the nape of my neck, a steady pressure that makes me shiver, makes me boneless, and uses it to propel me out of the door and into the hallway. I barely notice the trip downstairs, couldn't tell anyone the color of the car he urges me into, but I can describe the weight of his hands, the heat of his skin on mine.

I don't even think to ask where we're going until the car is already stopping outside a little building with large windows, a riot of color behind them. The sign is small and relatively plain, just yellow letters on black in a language I can't read.

"Come," Master says as he slides out of the car and holds his hand out to me. I take it and allow him to tug me onto the sidewalk, where he tucks me under his arm. Together we walk into the building.

Immediately I smell flowers.

Everywhere I look is something green or growing — tulips and daisies and roses, even a row of sunflowers by the window. It's bright, way brighter than I expect, so I look up, surprised to see glass in place of a ceiling.

"It's a greenhouse," I breathe out in surprise.

"Go look around," Daddy orders, but can I call it an order when I was already rocked forward on tiptoes, barely restraining myself from doing it? As soon as the words are out of his mouth, I'm sprinting to the nearest flower bed. There's dozens and dozens of them, some built at waist height on top of tables, some in pots along the wall.

I drop to my knees to stare at the one on the floor by the window with the sunflowers, hands shoved under my armpits so I remember not to touch. They are so pretty with their yellow petals and black seeds, the largest flower head the size of my palm. *Still babies, then.*

A shadow caresses me, and I look up to see Daddy smiling.

I can't help but stare.

It's not that I didn't notice before how…how *pretty* he was, when he first bought me. I did. Of course I did. Now, though, now everything about him compels me. His hair, black as a crow's feathers, begs me to brush it out for him, to braid it down his spine or into a crown atop his head, fitting his status as my Alpha. And his lips… His lips silently order me to listen. To obey, like at any moment he'll issue an order and I won't be able to stop myself from doing what he wants.

It's weird how he is both everything I ever wanted — a home, a place to belong, a person to belong *to* – but part of me is still afraid. Not *of* him…not anymore. If he kills me, at least I know it will be an accident, and I realize suddenly that I, and my wolf in turn, have deemed that an acceptable risk.

What scares me is how suddenly and fiercely I've grown attached, when at any moment he can send me away, cast me aside for a new feeder, a new lover…a new boy. I'm not special, I know I'm not. There's been no one in my life who has truly loved me, no one who has ever wanted to keep me.

Not my mother, not my old Alpha, not my old pack. Master, surely, will grow bored of me, too. It might be soon, it might be at the end of my contract, but he'll cast me aside and when he does, I'll be nothing — nothing but a broken toy abandoned by a careless child.

I shove away the reminder that my time with Master is limited, but it's too late. My ears start ringing and I feel like someone is tightening a belt around my chest in increments, tighter and tighter until I can't breathe. Master says something, but it's fuzzy under my panic.

I gasp in a breath as Master digs his nails into the skin of my upper arm. The bite of pain brings me back from the edge to see him crouched in front of me, his eyes concerned. "Eryn," he murmurs, and I feel like he's said it before.

"S-sorry." I stutter through an apology.

"What's wrong?" Master demands an answer with the set of his jaw.

"I just...I really like you." The words aren't anguished but my voice is, because I know it won't matter. I didn't even mean to say them. He drew them out of my throat like venom from a wound.

He smiles. "I really like you too, baby. Is that what caused this?" He gestures to my arm, still wrapped around my waist, clenching my shirt in tight fingers. I loosen them instinctively and look down as I nod. He tips my chin up. "Don't be scared, baby. I'm not going anywhere."

He lets me kneel in front of him for a long, calm stretch of moments before he guides me up onto my feet. "Come on. There's someone I'd like you to meet." He takes my hand and I follow. *Of course I follow. I'll always follow.*

Now that I'm not entranced by flowers, I hear the sound of someone puttering around in a back room, mumbled words interspersed with laughter. Daddy knocks on the doorframe of the entrance to the next room and a feminine voice invites us in.

The voice belongs to a dryad. Her skin is brown, with darker, almost-black markings like a tortoiseshell. The tips of her long fingers and ears are as green as her knotted hair. She gives Daddy and me a bright smile in greeting. "Prince Leviathan! Welcome!"

It is the second time I've heard someone call him 'prince', though I was too distracted by the atmosphere the first time to pay much attention, but it doesn't surprise me. Not much, anyway. My Daddy has a commanding presence, an aura of dominance and entitlement that goes hand in hand with power. I don't know what he's the prince of, and I find I don't much care.

"Little wolf, I'd like you to meet Chelone. Chelone, this is Eryn." Daddy urges me forward but stays close to my side, a comforting presence as we approach the stranger—a stranger to me, anyway, since Daddy obviously knows her.

Chelone smiles at me, her teeth yellowed with age and rot, though by her skin I'd thought her younger. It's hard to tell with dryads, though. They age with their tree, and in this world of technology and pollution, some fare better than others.

"He's a cute one. Likes flowers, does he?" Chelone asks, glancing at Daddy for confirmation. "I have just the thing. Wait here. Go ahead and water the scorpion grass. It's yelling at me for forgetting it. Such a little drama queen." Chelone rolls her eyes before heading up a flight of stairs, her shoes clicking on the tile.

I hurry to the five-petaled blue flower and water it before the dryad comes back and changes her mind. The forget-me-nots shiver under the thin stream of water, droplets beading on the silky petals, and I imagine they are grateful. Pushing just the tips of my fingers into the soil near the stems reassures me that I've given them enough.

"They like him," Chelone murmurs to Daddy. I jerk my hands out of the dirt and tuck them behind my back before I realize she isn't angry that I dared touch them.

"Bring him back in the summer, Levi. My dahlias will want to meet him."

She passes Daddy a leather satchel as she moves around him to stand beside me. Daddy tucks it into his pocket, and I quickly forget about it when Chelone takes one of my hands. Her fingers are stiff against mine as she guides it back into the soil.

"Feel that?" She closes her eyes and starts to hum, and I suck in a breath. I can feel the roots moving beneath the soil, tickling my fingers in greeting, curling around the tips like a little handshake.

Chelone smiles and leans in, lowering her voice but staring at Daddy like she knows he can still hear her. "If you get tired of *that* one, come find me, and I'll put you to work. My plants like you, which means *I* like you."

"Th-thank you, m-ma'am," I stammer, feeling my cheeks warm in a blush.

Daddy growls and steps toward me, gripping my biceps and pulling me tight to his side. "Stop trying to steal my boy, Chelone."

"Then best take care of him, Leviathan." She chuckles and reaches out to pinch my cheek. "For a possessive bastard, you're not great at taking care of your toys."

I duck my head, burying it in the fabric of Daddy's shirt. I'm not sure how I like being called Daddy's 'toy'. My dick stiffens in my pants, but an embarrassed tingle spreads like static over my skin. Daddy curls his hand over the back of my head, ruffling my hair. "Your concern is noted."

She harrumphs, and I hear her fiddling with something before she sighs. I sneak a peek and spot her glaring at one of the blue flowers. "You won't like it there," she snaps, apparently at the little plant. "It's hardly a good time for you to live in the wild, my dear, even if you *do* like him." She goes quiet for a few more seconds, then rolls her eyes toward Daddy. "Bring him back in the spring."

"I thought you said the summer?" Daddy asks, his voice teasing.

"Then, too, but the forget-me-nots want to go home with him."

Chapter Twenty-Five

Pet

Chelone lets me water a few more plants before Daddy says it's time to go — not, I suspect, because we have somewhere to be but because he is tired of the little digs Chelone keeps making. The bell rings above us as we step out onto the sidewalk. Daddy tucks me under his arm and guides me through the tangle of bicycles clogging the street to the waiting car.

"In you get, baby," Daddy opens the door for me and waits for me to slide across the street. He stretches over to help me snap my seatbelt into the buckle before he climbs in beside me. His hand lands on my knee and squeezes as he leans forward to talk to the driver.

"Now where are we going?" I ask, shifting as close to his side as the belt will let me get.

Daddy's smile is predatory. "Do you trust me?"

Immediately, I nod. "Yes, Daddy." Maybe it's stupid to trust the man who will likely kill me, but I don't care.

I'd rather live happily with him until it happens than go back to being alone. At least if I die, it will be meaningful...my blood literally prolonging his life. Maybe a small part of me will live on somehow, inside him.

Daddy doesn't seem to notice my melancholy thoughts at least. His smile widens. "Good, baby, because I think you'll *love* this."

Central Park isn't a dinky square of greenery tucked between skyscrapers and slums like I imagined it to be, the few moments I'd given it any thought at all. Daddy holds my hand as we stroll down the path, keeping me from stumbling. I stare up at the ancient trees, mouth open and eyes darting from side to side. I don't even know where to look. I can feel the energy dancing in the air, old and powerful.

"It's so big," I breathe, finally looking back at Daddy.

"Come on. I want to try something." He tugs on my hand, leading me off the paved path, into the shadow of the trees. A handful of steps in, he stops me, pushing me back against a trunk. The bark is rough, even through the fabric of my shirt. He drops to his knees and grips my right ankle, lifting it off the ground to unlace my boot. He tugs it free and drops it, then peels off my sock. He repeats the process with the other until I'm standing barefoot on the chilly dirt.

It's cold, and I don't even care. I flex my toes in the soil, relishing the feel of the dirt under my soles. Daddy trails his fingers over the tips of my toes, then over the arch of my foot to my ankle, stopping at my calves. He leans forward, pressing his face to my belly, nuzzling under the hem of my shirt until his lips are on my navel, licking and sucking until I no longer feel the bark or the grass or the nip in the air, nothing but his lips and tongue.

He teases me until I cry out, then pushes to his feet with a dirty grin. "Do you still trust me?"

"Yes, Daddy." I nod rapidly. Anything he asks of me, I'll do it.

"Take off your clothes," Daddy orders, and I shiver at the heat in his voice.

"People might see…" I say, but I'm not sure I'm worried. The thought that someone could stumble on us has me throbbing. I think Daddy can tell, because his smirk widens.

"I know." He strokes over my collar, and he might as well be gripping my dick. "Be a good boy and show me your pretty body."

"What if I get cold?" I ask, but I'm already tugging my shirt off with shaky hands.

"I'll take care of you, baby. You won't be cold for long." Daddy takes my shirt from me and folds it neatly, setting it on top of my boots against the tree trunk. "Now your pants."

I shove them slowly down my hips and he catches them before they land in the frost, holding me steady while I step out. He folds them as well, then slides his palms up my legs and over my thighs, dancing his fingertips over the lacy panties he'd dressed me in this morning. "Love how these fit you, sweetheart," Daddy murmurs, leaning forward to brush an open-mouth kiss against the fabric where it strains over my dick.

"I… Do you want me to l-leave them on? O-or…" I stutter, throwing my head back against the tree when he pulls the waistband down a scant inch to lick over the crown of my cock, which is already leaking.

"I'll take care of you, baby," Daddy murmurs and slowly drags them down over my thighs and off. He doesn't put them with my clothes. Instead, he lifts them to his nose and drags in a breath, smiling up at me as he takes in my scent. I moan and the sound stirs him. He stands and shoves my panties into his pocket, then steps closer.

He throws off heat like a furnace, hotter than any wolf I've stood near, and it staves off the frigid air. His hands, when he plants them on the tree, bracket my head as he leans closer. "Are you cold now?" Daddy asks, the tip of his nose barely skimming over my cheekbone to my ear, then down my neck.

I tip it in offering but he doesn't bite, he nuzzles, then seals his lips over my scent gland. He sucks, and it draws a whimper from my throat, which in turn pulls a chuckle from him. When he releases me, I know he leaves a bruise behind, another mark of ownership.

He cups my ass and lifts until my groin is level with his, rocking me against the zipper of his black jeans. It is just shy of painful, but that only pushes the pleasure higher. I barely notice when he starts carrying me deeper into the forest, to a snow-kissed meadow. The grass is frozen, crunching when he lays me down atop it. The snow melts where he plants his hands in it.

"Would you let me fuck you here in the snow?" Daddy asks, shifting to his knees to plant his hands on my thighs. They are hot enough to leave my skin pink, and it makes me wonder if his dick is that hot as well…and what that would feel like inside me.

"Please," I gasp as the thought appears, and I can't get rid of it. He's already so big, the stretch a burn of its own… Add in the fiery heat of his flesh… I shudder, almost coming untouched.

"Someone likes that, hmm?" Daddy purrs. He pushes my thighs open wider, and I can feel my hole clenching as he stares at me, like it too is begging. "Hold yourself open for me, baby." Obediently, I grip behind my knees and pull them back toward my chest.

"Good boy," Daddy grins down at me. He brushes the tip of his thumb over my hole in a teasing circle. No matter how I tip my hips, I can't get him to slip inside. "You're so tight, baby. Think you can take me without lube?"

I nod, not caring that it might hurt. I'm too far gone to think of anything but him taking me, claiming me...fucking me hard into the snow and dirt. "Please, Daddy, need you."

"So pretty when you beg." Daddy finally presses his thumb harder, sinking into my body with only a little resistance. It is thick and long, and I cry out, my back arching at the nip of pain. Slowly, he fucks it into me until I'm pleading for more. He replaces his thumb with two fingers, then three, and the stretch is almost too much and still...not enough.

"More, Daddy, please. I want *you*. Want your cock. Stretch me out on it, Daddy, please," I ramble, whining as I rock my hips, riding his hand. He pulls his fingers free, and I clamp my thighs around his in an attempt to keep him inside me. He dips his hand in the snow, melting it until his fingers are soaking wet.

"Sh-h, don't worry, baby. I won't leave you empty." He returns just the tips of his fingers to my ass as he shifts forward on his knees, his other hand making quick work of opening his zipper. He pulls out his cock, and my mouth waters at the sight. Then, he replaces his fingertips with the crown of his cock, thick and insistent.

It's as hot as I imagined, and I wait for him to push in, but he doesn't. He stays still until I whine, wiggling my hips. Daddy's laugh is dark and teasing. "Needy boy. You're so fucking tight, sweetheart. You grip my dick so good." Slowly, he sinks into me. He's as hot as fire and as hard as steel, and I can feel every centimeter he gives me. It hurts, but the look on his face, the twisted pleasure, makes it better.

It starts snowing, but the heat of our bodies has it melting on our flesh, mingling with our sweat. "Daddy!" I curl my legs around his hips, planting my heels on his ass to try to pull him in closer. I want to meld him to my body. Want him to climb inside me and *live* there.

His balls finally press against my ass as he spears me to the hilt, and I moan, clenching down on his dick like I can somehow hold him there. He chuckles, his breath hot against my neck as he collapses down against me, chest to chest. I hear the grass crunch as he fists his hands against it.

I don't think it can get any better, but then he does something with his hips that has his dick pressing that special spot in my ass like a fiery brand. I cry out, my hips arching. My cock rubs over his abs in an accidental tease. Pleasure jolts through me and my whole body twitches. "Daddy, do that again!"

Daddy's laugh is strained but he does, and I feel like screaming. "Bossy baby. Don't worry... I'll give you...what you want."

I feel my body shaking as I try to stop myself from spilling without permission. "So close, Daddy."

"Me too, baby. Come for Daddy. I want the woods to hear you scream." He does the thing with his hips again and it pushes me over. I climax with a yelp, cum coating my belly. Daddy slides his hand between our chests, splaying his fingers in my seed and rubbing it into my skin. He breathes against my neck for several long, peaceful seconds before he sits up, his dick still lodged in my ass. His hand stays on my belly, keeping me on my back.

His other dips into the pocket of his jeans and he pulls out the little leather satchel from the greenhouse. "I asked Chelone to make this for you. This one is a sample. She's sending the rest to the hotel room when she's finished with it." It's an abrupt change of topic, and I have a hard time focusing.

Breath wobbly, I clench on his dick as I ask, "What is it?"

"Do you trust me?" Daddy asks for the third time, and for the third time, I nod. He tips the satchel over into his palm. A ball of dried herbs rolls out, the size of a marble. "Lavender, adderwort...and aconite."

I bite my lip, fear swelling. Years of warnings and cautious tales war with my desire to please him. "Wolfsbane?"

Daddy nods. "I know it scares you. Will you take it anyway? Because I ask you to?"

My breath catches in my throat, and I close my eyes. I've heard all the stories of the addicts and abusers, of how easy it is to misuse, to take too much or too often. But Daddy isn't a stranger on the street, and he isn't a bully from my past. He wouldn't ask me to do something that would injure me.

My body is shaking—an odd feeling with his dick still lodged in my body—and my breath comes out harsh, but I open my mouth. The whole world seems silent, waiting, and then the bitter herbs are on my tongue. "Swallow for me, baby."

I close my mouth and struggle to swallow it. It's dry and I cough as it slides down my gullet. "Now what?" I ask, clearing my throat and grimacing at the taste, opening my eyes to meet his.

"Now we wait." Daddy moves, thrusting into me one last time after he comes before he pulls out, leaving me empty. I clench tight, feeling his cum try to work its way free, but I refuse to let it. I want it to stay. *Need* it to brand me from the inside out. Regretfully, I watch him tuck his dick in his pants before he drags me into his lap. The sudden motion has his seed painting my thighs.

"It'll help?" I ask, gripping his shirt tight like a security blanket, forcing my mind back to the conversation instead of the bitter loss of his essence.

"A few minutes and we'll know for sure, but I promise it won't hurt you. Worst case scenario, everything stays as is," Daddy says with a gentle smile.

"If it doesn't work, do I have to go back in the pen again?" I ask, my heart sinking as I realize how close the Goddess Moon is.

"No, baby, no." Daddy's hands tighten around me, and I feel my hair move, like maybe he kissed it. "You never have to go in the pen again, I promise."

"Okay." My voice is a whisper against his shirt. Daddy rubs my back, and we sit together silently. I feel when the herbs start working. My skin grows hot and tight, and I wiggle on Daddy's lap as I start to itch. "It's…um. Something's happening?" Everything gets sharper as the colors wash out.

"That's good." Daddy squeezes me tight, then helps me off his lap. "Kneel in front of me, baby. We're going to breathe together, okay?"

"Okay." I match my breaths to Daddy's, drawing in air when he does, releasing it slowly.

"Close your eyes. Good boy," Daddy murmurs when I do. I startle slightly when he clamps his hand around the nape of my neck, just over the collar. "I reached out to someone from the local pack. He assures me that you *will* be able to change, even outside the full moon. All you need to do is reach out to your wolf in *here*" — Daddy presses his other hand to my chest, right over my heart — "and coax him out. Stop fighting him. I know it's scary to give him control, baby, but I'm right here. All you have to do is trust me — and trust *him*."

I don't know how Daddy, who isn't even a were, could reach into the core of my fears and rip it to shreds so quickly, with so few words. It has always felt like a power struggle, the relationship between my wolf and me...like he knows I am terrified of him. Maybe it's my mother's words, circling in my head. *Monster. Beast. Dirty mongrel.*

Daddy makes me feel perfect, and with him here, I don't feel scared anymore. Daddy won't let my wolf hurt anyone. Daddy won't let my wolf hurt *me*. I squeeze my eyes closed tighter and, tentatively, reach out to the wolf inside.

Chapter Twenty-Six

Daddy

Three breaths later, and my hand isn't clasped around my boy's nape. It is buried in the ruff of his snow-white fur, still just over his gold collar. He is soft as silk when I offer him a scratch. Eryn's eyes, still blue, pop open, then his muzzle opens with a series of high-pitched yips. His fluffy tail wags, and he crouches playfully.

"Look at you, little wolf," I breathe, awed by the loveliness of his four-legged form. Sleek and muscular, he's still tiny, all legs and puppy energy. Eryn prances back and forth, dancing until he sees his tail. He chases it in circles, and I chuckle. It's clear that even with the herbs, my boy isn't in control, but his wolf doesn't seem violent like the feral ones I've met. Young, definitely, and energetic.

It makes me wonder...I lean forward. "Eryn," I snap, unleashing a thread of my tightly coiled aura to fill my voice with command. He freezes, then his head cocks, his ear twitching. "Come here, boy."

There's a second of hesitation, then he takes a step forward. When I don't move, he takes another one, until he is standing, quivering, in front of me. "Sit, sweetheart." Slowly, Eryn obeys. I reach out and scratch his ears. "Do you understand me, baby? Give me a yip."

Eryn barks, his tail wagging, and I grin. "Good boy." I push myself to my feet and laugh. "Catch me if you can." Without waiting, I spin on my heels and take off into the woods at a sprint. I know better than to lead him too close to the walking paths, but the park has sprawled across over a thousand acres. We have plenty of room to run.

I hear his paws in the snow behind me as he gives chase. He is clumsy but fast. I hardly have to slow for him to keep up. As we approach a hill, I put on a burst of speed. Near the top, I duck between a tree and crouch. I can hear him crashing through the underbrush after me and as he sprints past, I leap out, catching him by surprise.

He yips as I grab him, my arms curling around his sides to cushion his fall. Playfully, I growl and bury my face in his neck, clamping my jaws gently around his throat. Immediately, he goes limp, his head falling back and belly exposed, completely submissive. *Mine mine mine…*

He lets me play with him — gripping his paws to massage the soft leathery beans of his toes, tugging on the strip of hair sticking up along the center of his belly. Even when I unclamp my jaws, he doesn't get aggressive. His head stays back, his tongue lolling from his jaw and blue eyes soft.

"Such a good boy."

For hours, we play, rolling through the snow, chasing each other, until he flops down on his side near the meadow where we started. His stomach moves quickly as he pants, and I can't resist. I kneel beside him and curl my fingers in the fur, scratching the velvety-soft skin.

Then, without warning, his body shifts from wolf to human, flowing smoothly as his bones break and mend. In the span of less than a minute, my boy is blinking up at me, his lower lip clamped between flat human teeth. "We...we did it!"

"*You* did it, baby." He looks so happy I want to take him again, slide inside his hot little body and live there, but worn out and in skin again, he's shivering. "Let's go get dressed, sweetheart."

His clothes are right where I'd left them. He pulls them on quickly, but I find it sexier than any striptease I've seen. Those are things *I* picked out, that *I* bought him. I can't help that my thoughts immediately go to stripping them off him later.

He's halfway through tugging on his shirt when he freezes, his eyes darting toward the trees, wide and wary. I follow his gaze, my skin prickling, but see nothing. "Everything okay?"

"Yeah, I just...felt like someone was staring at me," Eryn says, lifting his hand to shield his eyes from the sun. "I don't smell anyone though..."

"I can go check, if you want," I offer, even though I don't hear anything but wildlife, like the squirrel gathering nuts in the nearby maple tree.

"No, I think... Can we just go home? To the hotel, I mean?" Eryn turns his eyes back to me, his gaze pleading. I'd think he was scared, if not for the tent in his pants.

"Yeah, I think I can find something for us to do." I wink. His cheeks blossom pink. "Oh sweetheart," I sigh, "the things you do to me with that pretty little blush."

Chapter Twenty-Seven

Daddy

The door to the hotel room clicks shut, and I have him stripped and on the bed without even bothering to turn the lights on. With my night vision, I don't need them, and the thought that I can see every constellation of freckles on his skin while he sees only darkness has me throbbing. He can't anticipate where I'll touch him...or when. Can't do anything but lie still and *wait*.

His eyes are open wide, straining for any speck of light, his mouth parted in a quick gasp. I move quietly as I kneel over him on the bed, careful not to touch. I want the first touch to be a surprise. I want to hear him gasp and watch his body arch. Want to see him chase the pleasure.

His breath is fast. I've never noticed a feeder's breathing habits like this before—unless it was that it had stopped, and except for the immediate regret, it didn't *affect* me, not the way Eryn's breath catching in his throat does. I can see his pulse fluttering, *hear* the blood coursing through his veins—even smell it, if I breathe in deep—but my desire to taste his seed is stronger than the urge to bite him.

Which isn't anything I ever thought would happen to me.

So rather than sink my fangs into his neck, I lean down and purse my lips, blowing a stream of air against the scent gland at the crook of his shoulder. Goosebumps spring up at the gentle breath. He moans, his head falling back, and the smell of his arousal grows stronger. I know if I reach down, I will be able to gather the pre-cum leaking from his dick like a faucet.

Instead, I finally touch him, settling my ass down on his abs like a weighted belt, pinning his hips to the bed. He whimpers, and I grin at the plaintive plea. I feel every twitch of his muscles below me, and I find myself wanting something I haven't in a long time.

"I want you to tell me something, darling. When you were alone in your bed, did you ever touch yourself?" I rock my hips over his trapped dick.

My little wolf turns scarlet, whining in lieu of an answer. My grin spreads, and I know he can't see it, but he doesn't need to. I'm sure he can hear the dark amusement in my voice as I say, "Go on, baby. Tell me what you dreamed of when you touched your little dick."

"I...I... Daddy, it's *embarrassing!*" He turns his head away, teeth digging into his lip and something about his shame turns me on even more.

"Tell me all about it, every little detail. I want to hear everything. And, while you do, why don't you show me how you touched yourself?" It takes only a second to flip on the lights, not because I need it to see, but I want *him* to see *me* — to look me in the eye with that embarrassed expression as he brings himself to the edge of climax then watch as I stop him just shy of release.

I move back to rest on his thighs. "Go on," I prod when he hesitates. "Tell Daddy your deepest desires." With a grin, I reach for his dick and give him a stroke. "And don't neglect the little guy while you do."

His whine is so embarrassed I can literally almost feel it teasing my skin like an erotic massage.

"I…I imagined someone kissing me…" Eryn admits.

"You're forgetting something," I interrupt, reaching out to grab his wrist, guiding his palm down to his cock and helping him curl his fingers around it. It might be *his* hand around his dick, but it's mine moving it. "There you go… Keep touching yourself, baby. You imagined a kiss, sweetheart? Where? On these pretty pink lips?" Tracing the fingers of my free hand over them has him shuddering. His strokes try to slow but I don't let him. I want him on edge.

"On my lips. And…and my neck, and…maybe on my…my…"

"Say it, Pet. Tell Daddy where you wanted him to kiss you."

His whole body starts shaking, his eyes already glazed. "My penis, Daddy!"

"Mm, and you *do* taste delicious. What else did you dream of, baby?" I abandon his lips to tweak his nipples into hardness.

If his skin gets any redder, he might combust. The tip of his dick is purple and soaking wet, and his chest heaves. "I…I like the way you stretch me, Daddy. I used…used to imagine being knotted."

I let my hand slow at the admission, leaning forward with interest. "Oh, *really?* And where did you hear about *that?*" Wolf shifters, despite the many fanfictions strewn across the net, don't knot. No shifters that *I* am aware of can. It's a fantasy, nothing more. But if my dirty boy wants to play pretend, I have plenty of toys...

"I read a story..." Eryn whines, head tossing back and forth. The tendons in his neck are tight and strained.

"Naughty boy, reading dirty books. Someone should spank you..." I tease and move his hand faster again. It earns me a whimper as his breath catches in his throat. "Maybe later," I concede, not willing to stop the play yet. "You like the thought of being stretched out, sweetheart? How much would you take for me, darling? Three fingers? Four?"

"Whatever you want, Daddy!" He's so blissed out that I could get him to agree to anything at this moment.

"How about my hand? Would you let me wear you like a glove? Pet you from the inside?" His body jerks hard enough that he almost bucks me off and I freeze, thinking it was enough tip him over by accident but, by some miracle, his dick stays hard and throbbing. "Oh, good boy, you *like* that, don't you?"

"Can't say that, Daddy. I'll come!" he begs.

"No, you won't, because Daddy said you couldn't. Daddy wants to watch his pet play with himself. You wouldn't want to disappoint me, would you?" My words are teasing. He doesn't answer, but I don't need one. My good boy doesn't want to disobey me. "Look how hard your little dick is, sweetheart. You're leaking so good. Feel how slippery you are? Tell me, when you were lying in your bed at home, all alone, touching your naughty little cock...did you ever consider topping?"

My boy doesn't have a dominant bone in his body but that doesn't matter to me. I've never considered bottoming to be *submissive*. Dick in my ass or not, I'm *always* in charge. The idea of riding my boy's cock like my own personal dildo is as sexy as hell.

My boy must like it, too, because he tears his hand out from under mine, fisting his fingers in the sheets as his dick twitches. I smell copper and moonlight, my gaze fixing on the small ruby bead welling up in his lower lip. I tug it free from his teeth, swiping my thumb over the blood before lifting it to my mouth. I make a show of it, my tongue cleaning it slowly. "Tastes so good, baby, but you never answered me..."

"You...you mean you want...you want *m-me* t-to..." he stutters, and I can tell he never thought it was a possibility.

"I want *this*..." I give his dick a squeeze, "in my ass. I want to pin you to this bed and ride your cock like my perfect little toy. I want your cum in my ass and mine down your throat."

His eyes are black with want, the pupils blown and lids wide. "Tell me if you want it, sweetheart. Use your words or I'll think you don't. Want me to bring you off with my hand instead?" I reach for his dick like a threat.

"No!" Eryn cries, moving almost instinctively as he grabs my hand to stall it, a more demanding move than I've ever coaxed from him. Any other lover, I'd be pissed, forced to punish them for the disrespect. Eryn, though...it only makes me grin.

"Something wrong, darling?" I tease, twisting my hand in his grip to dance my fingers along his forearm.

KD Ellis

"I want…*that*. I want what you said, my…my little dick in…in your ass, Daddy. Please, I… It's so hot, want you…" His words are nearly slurred with pleasure.

I shift forward, hovering over his hips, then take his wrist to guide his hand beneath me. "You won't hurt me. Give Daddy two fingers to start." I love the way his breath speeds up as his fingertips brush, soft as feathers, over my ass. "Go on, baby. Don't tease Daddy." He presses harder, and I feel my ring give beneath it. His hands are so tiny, my pretty little wolf… Two fingers is barely a stretch. "Good boy. I can take another one…"

"I… Should I use lube?" Eryn asks nervously, and I break my smile a bit more gently than he's used to, surprised to find myself touched by the courtesy. I'm a *demon*. Pain isn't something most people have worried about with me.

"I don't need it. You're leaking so nicely for Daddy, aren't you? It's like your dick knows exactly what I need." I give him a stroke as a reward. "Tell me that you want it, baby. Beg to fuck Daddy's hole."

His breath is rapid as his voice bursts out. "Please, Daddy, I want it, I want to…to fuck your…"

"Say it, baby," I urge, wanting to hear his sweet, innocent voice saying the dirty words.

"I want to fuck your hole," he blurts, *finally*, when I'm so keyed up that I want to sink down on him anyway. The words are barely out when I'm dropping down onto his dick. As much as I tease him about his little cock, he's well-proportioned for his frame, and the stretch is nice—more than pleasant, even just the physical sensation. It's the look on his face though, the *rapture* that crosses it, that really does it for me.

I don't tease him the way I normally would, purely because he's already so close to spilling that I know he couldn't hold off. I find that I don't want to torture him. I want to make this *memorable* for him…something I've never cared for before.

Eryn is *special*.

"Feels so good, little wolf," I praise, circling my hips so his dick hits my prostate like a homing beacon. He moans and clenches his eyes shut, which makes me still. "No, baby, open your eyes. Watch Daddy take your dick. Don't you want to see how good you make me feel?"

"Yes," he whines, and his hands twitch like he wants to reach for me.

I lean forward and grab his wrists, dragging his hands up to my chest, guiding his fingers to my nipples and urging him to pinch them. He does but it's hesitant, hardly enough to sting…and still somehow perfect. I'm not sure anything he does could be anything else.

Curling my fingers over his, I press down hard, then show him how to dig his nails into my skin — over my chest and down my abs — just the way I like. "Daddy?" Eryn asks, and there's something different about his voice. A vulnerability that seeps through the words like a cold wind under a cracked door. "This means something, right?"

"Of course, baby," I answer immediately, letting go of his hands to press one of mine to his chest.

"I mean…" Eryn bites his lip. "Never mind, I'm just being silly."

"Sweetheart, are you asking for reassurances?" I press, patting gently over his heart. "You don't need to worry. You are *mine*, Pet. I'm not letting you go."

"Ever? I... Do I still have to leave? After this..." Eryn touches the gold collar, "goes away?"

"No." My hand, almost of its own volition, jerks up to press against the warm metal. My voice is a growl. "You're *mine,* pet. It won't be that easy to get rid of me." As nice as he feels buried in my ass, his words make me want to reassert my ownership of his body. I shift my thighs, letting him fall from my hole as I shove his thighs forward to open him quickly. I don't have the patience for lube, so I tear my forearm open with my teeth, coating my fingers in my thick, viscous blood. The wound heals before I've even speared him on my cock. He yelps. "*Mine,* little wolf," I repeat.

"Yours, Daddy, *please,*" he whines, his thighs flexing under my hands. "Don't wanna leave."

His words calm the near-feral monster swelling in my chest and, once I've sunk as deep into him as his body allows, I still, letting his thighs go to drop down against him, chest to chest. He is small and frail beneath me but his body writhes like a live wire. "Never gonna let you leave, baby."

My earlier restraint snaps, and I bite him — not even to feed, just to claims him as *mine* – going so far as to scrape my nails up his chest and over the other side of his neck to add a few more marks. I slip my fingers into his mouth, wanting to be inside as much of his body as I can.

"*Mine,*" I growl again as I finally unclamp my jaw. At the same time, with a vicious thrust of my hips, I bury myself as deep as I can. Several rapid snaps of my hips tip him over and he screams, loud and nearly anguished. Cum splatters my abdomen and his, and I let myself go, filling him with my seed. "Always, *mine.*"

"Yours," he agrees, his voice ragged.

Chapter Twenty-Eight

Daddy

I'm still inside my boy when my phone rings. It's somewhere in the pocket of my pants, discarded on the floor between the entryway of the suite and the bed. The old me — the me before Eryn — would have pulled out and answered it. Instead, I continue running my left hand down my boy's side, probing the velvety warmth of his mouth with three of the fingers on my right.

I'm tracing each one of his dull ivory teeth when it rings the second time.

The third, I'm buried in his body again.

It doesn't ring a fourth time.

* * * *

Glass shatters and a chill spreads quickly through the room. *A window*, I realize, rolling off the bed. I drag Eryn with me, shoving him to his knees between the bed and the nightstand, hopefully out of sight. I am nude, my weapons in their bag by the front door. I have no hope of reaching them in time.

Thankfully, I don't need them. The monster inside is ready to come out, and by the time the Whisper strolls into the bedroom, its mouth gaping in a needle-sharp grin, I've unleashed it. I've heard my wings likened to those of a bat and my horns to those of a ram. Neither is even close to describing their true splendor. I've stared at my reflection in the mirror. I know what my monster looks like, and it is beautiful.

Beautiful, but deadly.

I meet the Whisper with claws and teeth. The demon is fast, avoiding the vicious flurry of blows I aim at him. Acid floods my stomach as the Whisper ducks the assault and lands his own, shredding my chest from rib to hip. I can feel my flesh stitching itself together but it's not the pain that worries me.

My boy is defenseless in the room behind me. I can't risk the Whisper getting past me, which limits my attacks.

It's been so long since I've felt fear that I forgot what it tastes like.

He's faster than me, but I'm stronger. It's too evenly matched here, with my boy at risk.

I step back, wings unfurled to block the doorway to the bedroom, and lower my claws slightly. "Whisper, I will give you one chance. Leave, and live to meet another dawn."

"My Masssster has given me a tasssssk," the Whisper hisses, forked tongue slipping between the sharp teeth like a snake. His claws lift to his throat as he tips it, scraping at the sigil carved into the flesh. "I mussssst obey."

"You must know you won't match me," I snarl, magic unfurling beneath my skin. Shadows stretch toward me, reaching toward my power. If the Whisper were a creature of mortal flesh, I could tear the blood from his veins.

The Whisper's laugh echoes against the walls. "I am jussst…the disssstraction."

Behind me, my boy yelps. Before I can spin, lightning spears into my spine. My chest grows heavy, and I look down. The sharp tip of a tourmaline stake sticking out of my flesh is all I can see. The skin around it calcifies, turning to stone in a far too familiar feeling. I stumble back, collapsing down to a knee.

I can't move. The spell won't kill me, won't even last long…but it'll last long enough. A heavy foot strikes my back, and I collapse to the side, smacking my face into the floor. Seconds later, terror fills me. Not for myself—there isn't a weapon in the mortal realm that could kill me permanently—but for Eryn.

A withered old man drags him out from his hiding spot beside the bed. Eryn's fingers scrabble at the man's hands but he can't free himself, and his face… It's white with fear. I want to beg for the man to release him, to take me instead. I can't move my jaw to speak. A gnarled hand fists Eryn's hair as the man yanks him along the ground toward me.

I don't recognize the man, not when he looms over me, holding Eryn like a ragdoll, not when he shoves my boy to his knees in front of my face—not even when his shriveled fingers grip Eryn's gold collar, sickly gray magic sparking against the metal until it shatters. Eryn cries as the gold shards scratch his neck.

I don't recognize the man until he gives me a familiar crooked smile. Puck grabs my pet by the hair and says, "Hello, *Daddy*."

Chapter Twenty-Nine

Pet

"Don't hurt him," I beg, scrabbling at the surprisingly strong hands holding me in place on my knees in front of Daddy. The old man tightens his fist in my hair and yanks my head back to a painful angle.

"Shut up, bitch," he orders. His voice is gravelly, like a lifelong smoker, as he forces me to meet his milky eyes. My throat closes as terror fills me.

My body shaking, I swallow. I feel naked without the collar, exposed and vulnerable. I was useless, a coward... I'd let my Master, my Daddy, my *Alpha*... fight that creature alone, then this...stranger had appeared out of nowhere, as if by magic — well, likely actually *by* magic — and I'd done nothing, nothing but *yelp* like a pup when the bastard stabbed Levi in the back.

The bastard in question leans in close behind me. I can feel his heat along my spine, and I shudder, my body arching to get away, but he doesn't let me. Keeping his grip in my hair, he runs his other one over my naked chest. Fury flares in Daddy's eyes but he doesn't protest, doesn't move, frozen like a statue.

"I heard you got a new pet, *Daddy*," the old man taunts. "Didn't realize he'd be this pretty." He yanks my head back even farther, and I yelp at the pain. His nose trails over the side of my neck, his breath moist and unwanted. "I'd only planned on using him as a sacrifice, but maybe I should play with him a bit."

The words fill me with even more terror, and I start to cry as I lose control of my bladder. Urine leaves a hot trail down my thighs. "Not even housebroken yet, I see." It's humiliating, kneeling in my own piss. Worse, knowing Daddy can see me, *smell* me, and there's no way for me to hide. "Say goodbye to Daddy, bitch."

I shake my head, biting my tongue to keep my mouth shut.

"Disobedient cur." Anger is a dark undertone in the man's voice, but I refuse to obey him. He's not my master, not even if he broke my collar, something that shouldn't have been possible. "Don't worry, Daddy," he snarls as he yanks me to my feet. "I'll break him for you."

My eyes lock with Daddy's, then air swirls around my skin, freezing cold. The world disappears around me.

It reappears, but everything is different. The man lets me go, and I fall to my knees on cold cement, in what looks like a dirty, foul-smelling warehouse. I scramble to stand but the man shoves me back down. "Don't bother trying to run. The exits are warded."

"Who are you? Why did you grab me? And…what's going to happen to Da—to Levi? Is he going to die?"

My voice breaks with the last question as a sob creeps up my throat. Tears soak my cheeks.

"Should have known he'd replace me with a crybaby," the old wix mutters darkly, crossing his frail arms over his chest. "*Daddy* will be fine, more or less, once my little spell wears off—which won't be quick enough to save you, so don't go getting your hopes up."

"Why are you doing this?" I ask, hoping to distract him enough so I can spot a way out. Unfortunately, he's right. Every exit I spot glimmers dimly red with magic.

"Why not? I suppose you think you're *special*. That you *mean* something to him. That *you'll* be the one to change him. I remember being that naïve once." He starts to pace, one of his legs dragging slightly. He turns abruptly and glares at me. "How old do you think I am?"

"I...I d-don't kn-know..." I stutter. A wix could live hundreds and hundreds of years and look in the prime of his youth, if his magic ran deep enough or if he didn't tap into it ever.

He scoffs. "Thirty-nine, *not* that you can tell." He gestures over his frail form. "I thought taking his *Focus* would slow...*this*. But look at me now. He stole my youth from me, then cast me aside. Wouldn't even give up something as *worthless* to him as a magic toy. He barely used it, anyway." His voice drops, like he's talking to himself now.

"You...were you one of his feeders?"

"Feeders? Of course not. Nasty business, that." His lip curls in distaste. "I was his *boy*...until I made a mistake. Just one little mistake, then the fucker tried to get rid of me. But I'll show *him*. Did you know"—he stalks toward me, darting his hand out quickly to grab me by the neck— "that in this very city is a weapon that can kill Death?"

I shake my head. It doesn't seem possible. I can't even wrap my head around the idea. He must be insane.

"Of course, Daddy keeps screwing things up for me, chasing my demons around the city." He glares at me like it's my fault.

Anger swells in my chest when he uses the word 'Daddy' again, like somehow he still has a claim on him. He's *mine*. He said so.

"Stop calling him that!" I blurt, anger taking over my mouth and, with it, my good sense.

"Shut up!" the man screams, then he's in my face, yanking my hair like a leash to shove me on my ass. "You think you *deserve* him? Little idiot, you're nothing more than a warm hole for him to dump his cum in. He's going to stretch you out, tear you up and drain you dry...then throw you out with the trash, just like he does with *all* his feeders. Didn't you wonder what happened to the others? Silly boy, you're *food.*"

A sob rips from my lips. I know he's right. It was always too good to be true. Daddy was never going to keep me forever. No one wanted me for long, not even other wolves. Still...

"You're right," I admit, steeling myself against the pain to meet his glare, "But if I don't mean anything not him, why did you take me? I can't get this...this so-called weapon for you."

"Daddy doesn't like to share his toys. You might be a passing fad, but he'll still be angry. Honestly, I could have grabbed any one of the homeless humans infesting this city. I just need a beating heart to activate the pashupastra. It doesn't have to be yours." His grin is wicked as he grabs my throat again. "I want him to *hurt* the way I hurt. Taking your pathetic existence away is the closest I can get."

He lets me drop to the ground as he steps back. "Sit tight, little bitch. My Whisper will be here with the final piece of the weapon soon. Enjoy your last few days of life. It ends on the solstice."

I'm afraid—terrified, really—but my inner wolf is whispering at me not to worry. *Daddy's going to save us.*

Chapter Thirty

Daddy

"Shit, Levi, what the fuck happened?"

If I could move, Aries would be staring at my middle finger. Unfortunately, the spell carved into the tourmaline is still holding strong. The most I can do is glare as Aries drops to his knees in front of me. His eyes widen at the sight of the stake. "Oh Levi, not again..."

I strain against the spell and manage to get a single finger to twitch. Not the finger I want, though, and Aries doesn't notice—which might be a good thing since I need him to remove the stake if I don't want to wait for the spell to wear off naturally.

Unfortunately, his hand is only halfway toward my chest when he freezes, his skin going pale as he glances around the room. "Where's Eryn?"

Power floods my limbs as rage and terror mingle in my bones, strong enough to loosen the spell by a hairsbreadth, enough to let a growl spill out of my throat.

"Oh." Aries cringes, guilt filling his features. "Shit." He digs his phone out of his pocket and presses a button, then holds it to his ears. "Captain? Yeah, I didn't get here in time. Leviathan is down, and a civilian is missing." There's a pause, then Aries says, "A werewolf, first name Eryn, last Laurier. He's Prince Leviathan's newly bound feeder." Aries winces. "Yes, ma'am. I understand, but... No, of course not. No, I don't want that, either. Yes, ma'am. We'll arrive shortly."

I don't like the look on Aries face...and my anger is justified when he grimaces and apologizes. "Sorry, friend, but we can't risk *two* demons rampaging through the city. I'll have to bring you to a containment cell, until we get everything sorted out, at least."

As soon as this spell wears off, I'm going to kill him — rend his flesh from his bones and use them as toothpicks. I'm not worried about the prison — those cells were designed with *my* input, and I have never been stupid enough *not* to leave myself a way out. I'll be free by the solstice.

I'd try to escape during transport — even tourmaline will wear off eventually — but I'll need a new *Focus* to go up against Puck. And I just happen to know that the nearest one is stored in the bowels of the BAA headquarters...right where they're taking me.

To get my boy back, I'll burn this city to the ground.

Want to see more from this author? Here's a taster for you to enjoy!

Demon Daddy:
The Blood Demon's Collar
KD Ellis

Excerpt

Pet

"Enjoy your last few days of life. It ends on the solstice."

The old wix's voice rattles around my brain like a pinball, making it hard to think. *The solstice?* I whimper as I realize it's only three days away, on the first night of Goddess Moon's visit.

"Oh, stop your whining. It's not like your miserable existence is worth much, anyway. You should be thanking me." The old Wix grabs for me, and I flinch back, but I only manage to scramble away a few feet. He's faster than he should be, considering his condition, and my hair is a liability.

He gets his gnarled fingers tangled in it easily, and he jerks me to a halt. It wrenches my neck and I yelp, lifting my hands instinctively to try to relieve the pressure. He drags me back toward him, a nasty smile on his face. "Go ahead. Thank me for ending your poor, cowardly little life."

I shake my head — or try to — tears spilling down my cheeks as I feel several strands of hair separate from my scalp. I'm not thanking him for this. I'm *not*, no matter what he does to me. I need to stay strong—for myself, but also for Daddy.

"You know," the wix muses, lifting his other hand to my face. His fingers are scratchy and rough, and they reek like rotten eggs. "Daddy *has* always had good taste."

Something about the way he says it makes the panic in my chest grow even stronger. I try again to pull away, but he clamps his fingers into my cheeks, keeping me in place. His nails are long and sharp.

"Stop squirming, dog," he snaps, and no matter how frail he looks, he's clearly stronger than I am. He uses his weight to push me down farther.

I'm forced to let go of the grip I had in my hair—the only thing stopping *his* grip from becoming unbearable—to catch myself, crying out as my palms land on something hard and sharp, like gravel.

Thankfully, he lets go of my hair. Before I can do more than breathe a sigh of relief, he slides his dirty, wrinkled fingers over my lips. I clamp them shut, biting my teeth together so hard my jaw aches.

"Open up, puppy dog. Show me your pretty pearly whites," the wix says in a creepy, sing-song voice. I try to shake my head, unwilling to open my mouth. I only budge it a fraction of inches, but it's enough to get my point across.

If he wants my mouth open, he's going to have to *make* me. I'm not doing it for him.

He just laughs. "So you *do* have a spine. I was beginning to wonder. I knew Daddy couldn't have changed *that* much in only ten years." The wix pauses, lowering his brows for a moment. "Eleven?" After a second, he shrugs, his rheumy eyes meeting mine again. "Either way, we're going to have fun together,

mutt. I've always wanted to play with Daddy's toys...
It's just a pity for *you* that I've never quite learned to
play nice."

Then he smiles, and every one of his yellow teeth is
a caution sign.

He shoves me again, forcing me to my back, then he
plants his foot on my chest. The tread of his boots bite
into my skin, reminding me of my nudity. I try to cover
my penis, but he shifts his foot to kick my hand away,
threatening to crush it under the heavy sole until I yank
it back.

"No point in hiding, dog. Not much there to hide
anyway, is there?" He stares pointedly at my crotch,
and despite the chill in the warehouse sending
goosebumps across my skin, I feel myself heat with
embarrassment.

I've been naked before, many times. It's a part of life
for us werewolves and not something I've ever been
ashamed of. But the only person who has ever looked
at me like *that* was Daddy, and it had never felt like *this*.
The derision, the judgement...making me feel small
and worthless.

Making me feel dirty.

A lump forms in my throat, threatening to choke me,
and I force myself to swallow it, though tears burn my
eyes. I need to stay strong for Daddy. Levi's going to
find me, and when he does, I can't be *broken*. He won't
want me then.

He won't want you now. The thought hits me too
quick to ward against, and my flinch is hard.

The wix laughs, grinding his foot on my chest again.
I try to dislodge him but I'm *weak*—too weak to fight
free from an old man. Maybe Beta was right all those
times he'd told me I was worthless, useless, a drain on
the pack resources.

Maybe I should have just let him kill me then.

Immediately, my wolf revolts inside me. I might feel like giving up, but he's not ready to die yet. He snaps his teeth at my ribcage, and I can almost hear him snarling at me to pull myself together.

"You're pathetic," I say, desperate to distract the wix. Maybe if I get him angry enough, he'll beat me instead. "No wonder Daddy didn't want you anymore."

His fingers freeze on the clasp of his dirty brown robe. "What did you say?" His voice sends ice down my spine, but I lick my lips and repeat myself.

"I…I said you're pathetic, and Daddy was right to…to kick you out. You're just jealous he doesn't want you anymore." My own voice is shaky, and I think he must realize I'm stalling for time, because the anger on his face morphs to a smirk instead.

"Aw, so the *widdle puppy* has teeth, does he? Leaving Daddy—and *I* left *him*, I'll have you know—was the best thing I ever did for myself. If I'd stayed, I'd be nothing more than his cumdump. Just a hole, like *you*. Now, let's see if *your* hole is as good for me as it is for Daddy."

* * * *

Daddy

The goons from the BAA are less than careful as they transport me down the elevator and into the black van waiting outside. Granted, my body is essentially living stone at this point, so the few knocks to the head I get don't hurt, but they *do* stoke the flames of my anger.

Every second they take to remove the tourmaline stake is a second *longer* it's going to take for me to metabolize the toxin and regain the ability to move—which means it's another second longer my boy is stuck with that...that...

I can't even think of a strong enough insult.

The Puck I saw today was not the one from my memories. If he hadn't dared lay a finger on Eryn, I might have felt pity for what he's turned into. When he'd fled a decade ago, he'd been a youthful twenty-nine, though even then I'd started to see the signs that he was reaching the limits of his magic.

I'd tried warning him, but he'd refused to listen, always pushing himself too much, too fast...using magic for things he could have done without. Always pestering me to borrow my *Focus*, then pouting when I refused.

Puck wouldn't listen when I tried to explain that the tool was only that...a *tool*. It could help direct magical energy more efficiently, but it didn't *create* magic. It still had to pull from *somewhere*.

For me, it isn't a problem. My own magic is boundless—gathered from the air around me and the blood I drink, replenishing itself faster than I could ever hope to use it. The *Focus* just lets me direct that energy into spells. Without it, I'm basically an overcharged battery, too powerful for anyone to tap.

For him, though... I suspect I know what happened. I'd bet my liver that he'd tried channeling too much energy through the *Focus*. Now look what it did to him—an old man at nearly forty.

I hate to think what he could be doing to my precious Eryn right at this second. He'd always been a jealous boy—and a selfish one, too. Constantly throwing tantrums, teasing the servants...anything he could think of to get my attention, except asking for it..

The final straw in our relationship had been when I'd caught him experimenting on one of my feeders in the hopes of stealing her magic. I'll never forget the poor selkie's face. She'd died shortly afterward.

He'd insisted it had been for 'research' and that the breakthrough would revolutionize magic use forever. I'd called it torture. If only I hadn't let my feelings for him blind me. I'd thought it love, then, but now after my time with Eryn, I'm not so sure. I'd believed him when he said he would go peacefully with the BAA for sentencing if I just kissed him one last time. Everything in me had said it was a bad idea, but I'd ignored my instincts.

Then, he'd staked me with tourmaline before stealing my *Focus* and fleeing, leaving me to rot. If Maggie hadn't found me the next morning, who knows how long it would have taken me to recover.

If he'd been willing to skin that poor selkie just to see what her magic would do, what is he doing to Eryn right now?

About the Author

KD Ellis is a professional cat wrangler by day, and an author by night. She moved from a small town to an even smaller village to live with her husband and wife and their two children. She loves reading—anything with men loving men. She writes queer romance in between working her two jobs and cuddling her pets—all six of them, which confuses the turtle.

KD Ellis loves to hear from readers. You can find her contact information, website details and author profile page at https://www.firstforromance.com/

Sign up for our newsletter and find out about all our
romance book releases, eBook sales and promotions,
sneak peeks and FREE romance books!

www.ingramcontent.com/pod-product-compliance
Lightning Source LLC
Chambersburg PA
CBHW020319260626
47156CB00004B/1287